The Yellow Ochre Stain

Books by Kee Briggs

The Third Removed
The Painted War
Finders-Keepers
Losers-Weepers
The Painted Lady
A Few Good Old Men

The Usher Orlop Mysteries

The Golden Janus/The Pewter Masks
The Nickel Trophy/The Bronze Bones
The Brass Portraits/The Zinc Ormolu
The Silver Scepter/The Rhodium Dragon
The Copper Shakes

The Asti Fantasies
Charm Catcher/Dream Weaver

ebook
Write To Live Longer

The Yellow Ochre Stain

A Sage Grayling Mystery

Kee Briggs

Keescapes Publishing

Satellite Beach, Florida

The Yellow Ochre **Stain**

Keescapes Publishing books may be ordered through booksellers or by contacting :

Keescapes Publishing
90 Flamngo Dr.
Satellite Beach, FL 32937
www.keescapes.com
KeescapesPublishing@gmail.com

ISBN 978-0-9820044-5-6

Published in the United States of America

The Yellow Ochre Stain

Kee Briggs

Chapter 1

Sage swatted the cement dust from his jeans before he folded his six-foot four-inch, slender frame behind the wheel of an old utility van. It seemed as if he was spending a lot of his time and a sizeable portion of his money at Builders' Supply. He had an endless list of things that had to be done to the ancient hacienda house ruins he had purchased outside of Albuquerque. Weather dictated his schedule: repairs had to be completed before it rained or it got too hot or too cold. But, even with the time and monetary pressures, he could still smile. He loved to wander around hardware and building supply stores. Such places had "things to make things with." And when he finished his project, he would have the most wonderful home and studio any trompe l'oeil artist ever had.

Large vehicles with tinted windows blocked his view in both directions as he started the van and slowly began to back out of his parking spot. He jammed on the brakes when an effeminate sounding horn began an insistent bleating. Through the back windows of the van, he saw a blonde woman shaking her fist at him. The action was accompanied by a shouted "ta ma de," which was a highly abbreviated form of an extremely vulgar Chinese expletive.

Sage leaned out the window to fire back, "Tudze"....*(rabbit)*. He stepped out of the van to get a closer look at the improbable apparition....a blonde yang kuaidze....(foreign devil)...swearing at him in Mandarin Chinese in the middle of the southwestern United States. Before he could exit the vehicle she had a response to his insult.

"Wanba dan"....*(turtles egg)*.

As Sage started down the alley between the vehicles, he could see the snout of a classic sports car.....bright yellow. When he stepped out into the open, he was confronted with an interesting spectacle. The blonde head he'd seen through the grimy back window of the van was attached to a stupendous body. A red, sleeveless blouse dove down, partially covering two boobs, the likes of which would normally be associated with a Frazetta painting. The blouse was tied just below those apparitions, revealing a small waist down past the navel. The lower extremities were covered with low-slung, form-fitting, faded jeans. That figure could find instant employment at any Hooters in the country or in any foreign country that the corporation may have invaded. She was standing with her fists on her hips, straddling the steering wheel of a 1952 MGTD.

A big grin spread across Sage's face when he rounded the front of the classic sports car. As he passed the front fender, he casually rapped it with a knuckle to see if it was fiberglass or metal. His gaze must have stalled somewhere above the exposed midriff, because the blonde said, "They're not fake and neither is the car."

Sage broke into laughter. "No one will ever believe me if I try to tell them about the big–bosomed, blue-eyed blonde, driving her grandfather's sports car, who cussed me out in vulgar Chinese in an Albuquerque parking lot. It's worth a beer to get the rest of the story. I'll buy you a cold one at Pedro's around the corner."

"You're on, cabron....*(goat)*, but not at Pedro's—the parking lot is too dusty. Make it Los Amigos down the block."

Sage wasn't sure how he should respond. He had just been called a nasty name....*goat,* in Spanish. He decided to hold any critical analysis until he found out more. He liked what he was seeing. "See ya there," said Sage, as he retraced his steps. The blonde slid back down into the driver's seat.

As soon as he cleared the front of the sports car, there was a satisfying, throaty growl, a small 'eke' of tires, followed by a cackle as the driver eased up to turn onto the main entry lane. By the time Sage was able to maneuver out of his parking space without hitting anyone, the distinctive MG roar announced the car's departure from Builders' Supply. At least, it had turned in the right direction. Sage had been half fearful the rendezvous was just a hoax to be shed of him. He found he was looking forward to seeing more of that stacked blonde.

The MGTD was parked directly in front of Los Amigos. When he stepped from the bright sunlight into the gloom of the bar, he paused for a moment to let his eyes adjust. A motion to his left proved to be his impromptu date. She was seated at the window booth directly in front of her shiny, yellow car. As Sage approached, she rose so she could look him straight in the eye. He was being measured.

Sage extended his hand. "Sage Grayling."

"Tinna Gunn."

Tinna had a firm handshake, but the offered hand itself wasn't what he'd expected. The skin was hard and callused. The nails were very short. But, that was the only thing he could see that was short. She was nearly as tall as he with the two-inch high heels on her cowboy boots. He was in sneakers.

"Shall we?" said Sage, motioning to the booth.

There were already two Tecates on the table with their requiite key limes perched on the can tops. A saltcellar sat between the cans.

"If you don't care for Tecate, order something else and then I'll have two," said Tinna with her first grin.

"This is my beer, too."

Both squeezed lime on the can lids and sprinkled salt into the juice. After a long, cool draught, both wiped lime and salt from their upper lips. "Now, tell me," said Sage, "how is it that a da pidza can swear like a Peiking coolie?"

"What's a da pidza? I don't know Chinese. I just swear in it," said Tinna with a shrug and a smile. "And how is it that a long, white fencepost like you knows what I'm saying?"

"A da pidza is a 'big nose', a common, derogatory term for foreigners. I was fascinated with Chinese, so I studied it. Why do you swear in it?"

"Some accuse me of having a foul mouth. I get into less trouble if those I curse don't know what I'm saying."

"Are you a local or just passing through? I've never seen your fancy little car around here...I'd have remembered."

"I just finished restoring it a few days ago. This is the first time it has seen the sun in a long time. By now, I suppose I qualify as a semi-local. I'm a holdover from the university. I decided I didn't want to go back to the ice and snow of Iceland, so I've set up my pottery here."

"Ah, a potter. So, you don't chew your nails."

Tinna jerked her hands off the table. "'Govnjuk'....(asshole). You really know how to hurt a girl, don't cha?"

"Nooo....just making an observation. I'd say you have sufficient reasons for not being a parts model for Revlon nail polish. What kind of work do you do?"

"I've been experimenting. I've found an engobe slip glaze that really excites me. It has two marvelous colors, depending on how it's fired. But, to bring out a truly unique color, I think I'll have to fire it as some of the Japanese did centuries ago. I can't do that where I am now. In fact, the neighbors are already screaming to the county commissioners about me having a gas kiln in the garage. It has something to do about zoning, or maybe it's the fire regulations." Tinna gave a little shrug and took another pull of Tecate.

"How did the Japanese fire their stuff?"

"In caves or bank kilns. It's called ana gama. Originally the potter dug a cave in a bank, put in a hole for a chimney, and built a wood fire in the mouth."

"That sounds like it could get expensive at the cost of wood these days. You'd think that lumber in the back of the van is made of gold."

"I plan on trying to fire it with cow chips."

Sage laughed. "Dung in the mouth?"

Tinna started to fire off another oath but caught herself and ended up saying, "Oh, you know what I mean."

"At least, there shouldn't be any scarcity of fuel in New Mexico."

"It's not as easy as it seems. I want the dried cow chips. I can't use the tons of it that's produced in dairy farms or feed lots where it's piled up in a heap. Gathering chips is a long, time-consuming business if you're going to do a lot of firing."

Sage had been making an analysis of his companion, as she was probably doing of him. Her light, blonde hair was just long enough to be gathered back and held with a rubber band in a tiny ponytail. If let loose, it would just crown her face...if fluffed up. Of course, she may wear the "just out of the shower look." That style didn't do much for him. She didn't have what one would call a pretty face, but it was attractive...more striking, than pretty. He came to the conclusion that as far as appearances were concerned, he wouldn't mind having her on his arm. So far, he wasn't sure about the non-physical attributes.

The waitress arrived with another round of Tecates in response to Sage's signal. After the lime ceremony, Tinna wiped her lip and said, "Well, I can see from your hands you don't do much physical labor. Are you some kind of pencil pusher....a thinker type?"

"I've never thought of what I do in those terms. When I work, it's long and physical, but there's not much weight involved, so I don't bulk up. Of course, there are other times when I sit around a lot to just think. That doesn't build any calluses either....at least where they show."

"Scheiße. (*shit*) With you, one can't be subtle. What kind of work do you do?"

"Oh, I'm a trompe l'oeil painter."

"A what?"

"Trompe l'oeil." I paint pictures on walls so it appears you are looking at a scene outside."

"Oh, I know what that is. I didn't know how to pronounce it."

"It's French....means 'to fool the eye'."

"I don't like French. I won't even swear in it. Are you with the university?"

"No, they pretend not to know me. I'm completely self-taught and that's a dirty word to that bunch. I've had people suggest I go through the process, pay the fees, and put in the time to get my pedigree so I can teach, but who wants to teach? I'm doing well enough without them, thank you."

"I don't recall seeing any work like that around here, unless you did the creeping vines on the Italian restaurant just off campus or the cartoon on the hardware store."

"I don't have anything out in the public around here. I did some museum diorama backgrounds in other cities, but most of my work is for private clients in their homes. That's usually much more fun."

"Do you make a living from your painting?'

"Now I do, but it was a long climb. The future keeps looking better. How about your pottery?"

Tinna grimaced. "I work for two big shows a year. Those keep me afloat. If I want any extras, I have to sell outside of those shows, which makes it difficult collecting enough for the shows. I'm hoping that my current experiments will produce something fabulously unique. That would put me over the top."

"If you could fire in a cave?"

"Well, nothing is for certain, but I hold high hopes. To run the experiments, I've scaled down the size of my pieces so that each failure doesn't destroy as many hours of work."

"Then, I take it," said Sage, "that you are not throwing on the wheel."

"Oh, no. I coil-build or slab-build most everything. I don't do utilitarian pieces. My work is much more sculptural. It's not sculpture, but it's decorative."

Sage took another drink of beer, giving himself a few moments to consider an idea that was floating around in his head. *Why not.* He said, "I have some acreage on the other side of the river. It's far enough out in the country that I have no neighbors in sight. There's a bank. You're welcome to run your experiments out there....if it's suitable."

"No scheiße, really? When can I see it?"

Sage had to swallow a snort at Tinna's language. "I'm headed home now. You can see it now, if you'd like."

"Great," said Tinna as she downed the last of the Tecate.

In the parking lot Sage said, "My place is off the paved roads. I rather doubt your pretty little MG will like the rough, dusty road. Do you want to drop it off at home? I'll bring you back."

Tinna hesitated a moment. Normally she'd not want to be without her own transportation, but her self-defense hackles hadn't risen, so she said, "Follow me and I'll drop Daisy off at my place."

Daisy, what a miserable name for a TD.

On the outer fringes of the university district, Tinna pulled off the street in front of a detached double garage with an apartment above. An opener signaled one of the garage doors. She pulled the MG inside and triggered the door button on the way out. Tinna climbed into the van and Sage headed west.

Civilization gave way to scrub-covered rolling land. Sage slowed to make a turn. As he passed a mailbox, he paused long enough to pull out a small pile of envelopes. A rather rutty, dusty road led around a small hill. Sage's comment about the road was that he needed to surface it, but it was rather low on his priority list.

Behind the hill was an enormous, old Mexican-style building. It was a squat one-story affair. Huge, double wooden doors were situated toward the left side. Periodically, tall, narrow windows with burglar bars pierced the front. There was an overall dun color to the structure, but in places off-color patches were evident and in other sections the outside skin had broken away, revealing large, dull red bricks. Attached to the left side was a new addition of fake adobe, sporting two oversized garage doors.

There were no real roads leading to the structure. Tire tracks wandered at will through the scrub brush. Sage veered off to the right.

"Scheiße, what is that?"

"That's the Lair?"

"What's a Lair?"

"Well, at the moment, it's not quite domesticated enough to be a house or a studio, but I'm working on it. I'm sort of camping in there and building it around me."

As they passed along the side, Tinna could see the structure was much deeper than it was wide. The first half had barred windows as along the front, followed by a blank wall and then another huge wooden door at the end. Through the back windows of the van she could see the rear was a featureless wall.

Sage didn't volunteer any further information about the Lair as he guided the van across the bumpy landscape. Tinna was risking neck strain trying to take everything in. Sage left the Lair behind in a swirl of dust as he headed toward a low hill. He drove out into a large, flat area about the size of a football field that had been carved out of the hill. There were piles of debris scattered over the surface. At the front edge of the area were the remains of a shed. The roof had fallen in.

"What is this place?" asked Tinna.

"This is where they made the bricks to build the hacienda house. Those mounds are the remains of the brick clamps.... where they built mountains of bricks and fired them. The brick makers just ate their way into the hill for their clay. It took a lot of bricks to build that building. The outer walls are almost three feet thick. They probably used dung as an additive to help fire the bricks. The molds were housed in that shed. Bugs and rot have done away with them, as well as the ceiling timbers. Are there any banks around here you could use for your kiln?"

"Sangre de Dios. I could dig a couple of dozen in here before the banks get too high." Tinna turned to look directly at Sage to see if he was putting her on. "Are you truly offering to let me build an ana gama here?"

"Yes, I wouldn't have brought you all the way out here to jut to tease you. You can use the site as much as you want. Don't cut down any trees to fire your kilns. There are precious few of them left. I don't have any cattle, so you'll have to collect your cow chips elsewhere."

Tinna still couldn't quite believe her good fortune. She was used to having to pay for whatever she got. Her skepticism was still showing. "How much are you asking?"

"Nothing. I'm not using that land now. I'm not deriving any income from it, so I'm not losing anything. I'd just like to see how your experiments go."

"You're sure?"

"I'm not even going to ask you to go to bed with me as a condition for using the site. It would probably be very enjoyable, but I don't do business that way. Later on, if your experiments turn out well and you want to get into any major production, then maybe we'll talk about some financial arrangement."

"Can I walk around to look things over?"

"If you like. When you're through, come back to the Lair. I have to unload the van. I'll leave the back door open."

Tinna started her tour of the site. Sage drove back to the house. The back door was actually two over-height wooden doors that swung out. Built into the left door was a passage door. Sage let himself in the small door to release the bar of the big doors. He drove the van into a room that had originally been designed as a granary. It would have easily accommodated five more vans. Building materials were stacked around the room. Light entered through bar less windows that faced into a courtyard behind the main house.

The potter hadn't returned by the time Sage had unloaded the building materials, so he left the door open into the courtyard and went on to the house. He wanted a cup of coffee. Diagonally across the courtyard was a passage into the main house. There was also a back door into a pantry and beyond it was the old kitchen. Sage hadn't done much to that room yet. It still had all the traditional features of a Mexican kitchen. He plugged in a hot pot to heat water. He was just pouring water over his Nescafe when he heard a "hello" from out back.

"Just follow the open doors," yelled Sage.

Moments later the blonde head appeared in the kitchen doorway.

"I'm making a cup of coffee. If you can stand instant, you're welcome."

"I can handle that."

Sage slid the cup along the counter as he reached for another. "If you want to add some spice to your life, stir your coffee with the spoon from that red jar. It's liquefied cayenne pepper."

"We don't grow chili in Iceland. I'm still only thinking about that hot stuff. I haven't gotten up enough nerve to try it yet."

"How many years have you lived in New Mexico? And you haven't tried our local cuisine?"

Sage poured another cup of water. He used a red-coated spoon from the jar to stir the brew. He got an angelic expression on his face after a sip. Tinna shuddered.

Looking over his cup, Sage said, "Will that site be of any use to you?"

"Oh, it will be perfect." Tinna was getting excited and she was slipping back into an accent which she had obviously taken pains to subvert. "The soil will hold a good, vertical wall. It's not easy to dig, but not impossible either. No one is close enough to complain...except maybe you." She raised her eyebrows.

"What would I complain about?"

"It might get to smelling a little like a barnyard out there, but not badly. There is a little smoke from the firing. Of course, I'll be coming and going."

"So far there's nothing that gives me any concern. When you drive in just beep the horn so I know it's you. I'll recognize that pansy horn. By the way, what will your little TD think about all this dust?

"I have a large stake-bed truck I use for this kind of stuff. That horn has balls. It's one that you can appreciate," said Tinna with a smirk.

Sage didn't quite know what she meant by that crack so he just motioned his guest to a chair at a small table that was almost lost in so large a room.

Tinna started to take notice of her surroundings. The long, high room was practically devoid of furnishings. Along the inside wall, between a couple of windows that opened into a courtyard, was a large, white refrigerator and an equally large upright freezer. The exterior wall was lined with a gaudy tile counter. Below the working surface was a series of small, arched openings for braziers. Above was a tiled hood with a vent through the ceiling. Toward the front of the house was an oversized tiled sink.

"Is this your kitchen?" she said with a laugh as she walked over to the counter to confront a long line of stark, white appliances. Starting at the far end she read the name tag, "convection oven." As she proceeded down the line she enumerated, "microwave 1, microwave 2, crock pot, bread maker, grill, rotisserie, rice cooker, fry pan, electric wok, hot pot. What is this, an appliance showroom?"

Sourly, Sage said, "You missed the food processor, blender, juicer, and spice grinder down below."

Tinna instantly recognized she had tread on some sort of sacred ground or tender spot. She retreated to socially stable ground while still not acknowledging any wrongdoing. "You've got to admit that is a rather strange kitchen."

"Yeah, it was even stranger a few months ago when there was no roof. I thought I was doing rather well to get hot water and electricity in here. Bring your coffee. I'll take you back to town. I leave for Los Angeles in the morning to give an estimate on a painting. I'll be gone for three days to a week, depending on how things go. You're on your own out back."

Chapter 2

Sage was up early the next morning. His bag was already packed. He took a quick tour of the house, making sure it was secure. He paused momentarily at the blast of a ballsy horn. Tinna was getting an early start too. Sage smiled and shook his head at the intriguing possibilities that now seemed to be wafting about the hacienda. He didn't have enough to time to socialize, so he tossed his bag into the van and backed it out of the garage. He wouldn't leave his Seville in long-term parking at the airport where the summer sun or vandals could work mischief upon it.

The short flight to Los Angeles was uneventful. He didn't even have time to get to the interesting part in his book. Flying wasn't the pleasure it once had been. Now it was test of perseverance, necessitated by autocratic stupidity and augmented by bureaucratic bungling. Homeland Security had more than doubled transit time between two points.

A mid-line rental car was waiting. By the time he cleared LAX and headed north along the coastal highway, he was in a foul mood.

Sage knew that his post-flight mental state would not be conducive to establishing a good, first-contact client relationship,

13

so he had arrived early. He would locate the address and then find a nearby motel with a good restaurant and bar. After checking in, he would enjoy a leisurely lunch and then relax until his 6:00 pm appointment. For some reason, his potential client, Dieter Brand, had requested a late afternoon meeting.

Finding the Brand house wasn't as difficult as Sage had expected. There were new developments rising up the slopes, but he didn't have to enter any of them. He stayed on the main road, winding up the canyon until he reached the top of the hill. Sitting on the crest was an imposing matriarch of a house with all the amenities of class missing in the ostentatious facsimiles that marred the lower elevations.

Having spotted his destination, Sage retreated to Coast Highway where he found adequate accommodations. He timed his return to the Brand home so he was driving through the gate at five minutes before the hour. He parked in the front portico. As he climbed the front steps with his art briefcase, the door opened. A casually dressed middle-aged man came out with his hand extended.

"Mr. Grayling, I'm Bert Mills, Mr. Brand's assistant. Please follow me. Mr. Brand is in his office."

As they stepped in the door, a chime clock struck the hour. Sage smiled. He prided himself on making appointments on time.

Bert smiled too. He knew his boss also valued punctuality. He led the painter through the entry and up a grand staircase to the second floor. The upper hall must have been twelve feet wide. Sage trailed his guide down the hall to double doors at the rear of the house. They entered a great room with an ornate fireplace directly ahead, surrounded by casual seating. To the right was a long board-room table lined with chairs. To the left, was a grouping of comfortable looking, leather chairs in a semi-circle around a massive desk. Seated behind the desk was a fiftyish, distinguished looking man, who was also dressed in casual atire. Sage felt overdressed in his conservative business suit. The man stood up and came around the desk to shake hands.

Bert Mills made brief introductions. "Sage Grayling, Dieter Brand."

Brand indicated a seat and returned to his position behind the desk. "Mr. Grayling, I'm pleased to meet you. I have admired the work you did for my friends, the Krugers. I have a little problem that I would like you to solve. Years ago, when I bought this place, I used to enjoy a splendid view out over pristine hills to the Pacific in the far background. In recent times, that magnificent landscape has been turned into an ugly sea of angular roof tops, antennas, and satellite dishes. You passed through them on the way up here. To avoid looking at that depressing landscape, I had the windows at the end of this room removed and a solid wall built.

Your job is to replace that horrid scene by painting the view out over the hills that I so fondly remember. Bert has dredged all the old photographs out of family albums and storage boxes showing the arched windows that used to grace this room and the view we could see through them. I would like to have the painting depict the afternoon sun as it would be about this time of day."

"That sounds as if it has all the earmarks of an interesting project," said Sage.

"Please provide me with a sketch of your ideas along with an estimate of the cost and the time involved. Bear in mind, I have an identical house in Dallas, Texas, with a similar problem. After completing this project, I would like you to work your magic there. Bert will show you around and give you all the particulars."

As Bert entered from the hall, Mr. Brand exited through a door behind the desk. The assistant must have been within earshot, or there was a hidden communication system. He carried a manila envelope to the board table where he spread out three or four dozen photographs. Some were old and faded.

"To give you a little history," said Bert, "this used to be what would now be called a family room. There is a matching room at the front of the house. It's the master bedroom suite. The two bedrooms on the west side....this side...are the children's rooms, and there are two guest rooms across the hall. This is where the kids played and the family gathered. There is a photo of the end of the room showing the wall, which was about two and a half feet high, below the windows and the two arched windows, which went nearly to the ceiling. At that time, there was other furniture and it was arranged differently."

"What was the window sill material?"

"Ummm, marble. Yes, brownish marble."

"The older photos don't show draperies," said Sage, "but those with the newer furniture arrangement have gathered draperies. Draperies or no draperies?"

"I'll check, but I suspect he doesn't want the draperies. They were installed after the Mrs. died. When she passed away, Mr. Brand never really felt comfortable in the master bedroom suite, so he moved into the bedroom across the hall. He had a private office built in the other end of this room and a door punched through to the bathroom so his bedroom, bath and office are joined together. The desk where he met you is for business meetings, as is this big table. As for the draperies, originally, there wasn't any need for them. The house was isolated and the windows were too high, but when Mr. Brand started using this room for meetings, he had to block out the afternoon sun."

Sage picked up an older photograph of rolling hills. There was a reflection in the glass of a young boy taking a photograph. "Is this the scene Mr. Brand wants portrayed?"

"Yes, but probably a little more to the right. If the atmosphere is clear enough, the Pacific is visible in the distance. Come, let me show you the view."

Bert led the way out of the big office into the first bedroom on the left. "This is Karl's room. Neither he nor his younger sister, Elke, are here very often." At the opposite end of the room there were French doors opening onto a narrow, railed balcony. Bert unlocked the door and both men stepped out into the setting sun.

Sage's artistic eye could filter out all the civilization clutter to get the impression of the scenic beauty Brand was hoping to resurrect. Once, it had been a spectacular view. A golden light was just beginning to tint the Pacific. In another hour, as the sun would drop toward the horizon there could be spectacular display of color, providing the air wasn't too full of gunk. Sage took note of the lighting. The sun was striking the top of the hills, leaving the depressions in a soft, subdued glow of reflected light.

Bert remained standing in the doorway. "Take all the time you'd like. When you get through, come downstairs. I will be in the room to the right of the front door. Please be sure to lock these doors otherwise when the housekeeper tries to set the alarm system, she'll have to run around the house looking for the open door."

A set of French doors from each of the two bedrooms opened onto the balcony. In front of each was a small metal, patio-style table and a couple of matching chairs. Sage laid out his briefcase to get a sketch book and a handful of colored pencils. He made a couple of quick sketches of the terrain without the houses. There were four discernable ridges. He would have to check the sketches against the photographs since there might be more ridges visible before all the construction. One of his main goals was to set the light and shadow patterns for this time of day. Having the sun shining toward the viewer was going to create a bunch of problems not normally faced by a trompe l'oeil painter.

Sage stayed until the sun was hitting him full in the face. When he went back inside, he dutifully closed and locked the doors. On his first trip through, he hadn't paid too much attention to the bedroom. As he passed through it again, he gave it closer scrutiny. It was probably twice the size of normal bedrooms, with higher ceilings....of course, nowhere near as high as in his bedroom. It was definitely a masculine room, although there wasn't much evidence of a strong personality. There were a few beer signs on the walls and hood ornaments on the flat surfaces. There were few books in the shelves and no sports memorabilia in evidence. Sage wondered whether this truly reflected Brand's son or whether the kid had removed all his treasures.

Bert was at a small desk putting postage on a stack of envelopes. He nodded to a chair as he continued his work. "What do you need to make your presentation?"

"I'll have to take the measurements of that room, review those photos you collected and take another look at the landscape when the sun is on this side. Will I be able to get in about 9:00 o'clock in the morning?"

Bert straightened his stack of envelopes and turned to give Sage his full attention. "Sure. In the morning, drive down the lane on the left of the house. It leads to the garages. You'll see a pipe rail and some steps. Park by the rail and go to the kitchen door. Mrs. Bruckner will be there to let you in. Anna is our cook whenever one is needed and she oversees the house. Since Mrs. Brand is dead and the kids are out on their own, we don't maintain a permanent staff. Oh, there are a couple of full-time gardeners, but no domestics. We have a professional cleaning crew come in once a week to do the maintenance. If Mr. Brand is in residence and there are guests, we have people that we can call to come in, as needed."

"Doesn't Mr. Brand live here?"

"He pretty much splits his time between this house and the one in Dallas. It's identical to this one. Mr. Brand likes to maintain a set routine. He wants to know where everything is located. The bathroom drinking glass is in the same place in both houses. His clothes are in the same order in an identical closet. Then he has various vacation spots around the country where he spends some time."

"You mentioned a couple of children, who are out of the house. If they still maintain rooms here, will I be likely to running into either of them while I'm here?"

"Probably not. Karl went to Rio for Mardi Gras and hasn't returned yet. He apparently hasn't gotten his fill of those thong bikinis," said Bert with a tinge of distaste. "Elke's in Texas right now. She's off on another of her ecological crusades. Since her father moved out of the master bedroom, she has pretty much taken up residence there whenever she does come home."

Sage noted another hint of disapproval when Bert spoke of the daughter. "Are there any coming events that I will have to consider once I start painting? I use oil paints and turpentine, which stinks things up a bit."

"No, Mr. Brand doesn't entertain much here anymore. He'd rather do it in a club or a hotel. You won't be interfering with anything that is currently scheduled. Of course, that is always subject to change. Come and go anytime. Mrs. Bruckner has an apartment behind the kitchen. She seldom goes out." Bert ran his eyes up and down Sage's frame. "Be warned, you're young enough and skinny enough to be in for a lot of mothering....but it's nice mothering. Neither Mr. Brand nor I will be here at 9:00. The photos are still on the table.

"Oh, one other thing, Mr. Brand said you can stay here at the house while you are painting. He is having Elke's old room made up for you. That way you can work on your own schedule. Please take that element into consideration in your estimate. Now, I have to run an errand before going home. I'll see you tomorrow."

Bert showed Sage to the door. On the way down the hill, Sage felt a sense of relief. Trying to land a commission was always a tense situation. Since his livelihood depended on getting clients, this initial phase was critical. He knew he could do the work once he got the job, but getting the job is the hard part. This time he hadn't even had to show his portfolio. The client had made his initial judgment on one of Sage's earlier works. The next phase would be to come up with a sketch giving the client what he wanted. Of course, there was always the financial consideration, but from what he had seen of the house, money probably would not be a particularly critical element in the final decision. Value had to be given, but in cases such as these, esthetics ruled over dollars.

The next morning, Sage parked by the kitchen, as instructed. He didn't make it to the door before it swung open, revealing a short lady with graying hair done up in a severe French roll. She gave him a frank appraisal from top to bottom.

"Mrs. Bruckner?"

"Mr. Grayling. Have you had breakfast?" The question came with a distinct German accent.

"Yes."

"Probably, a McMuffin and coffee," said Mrs. Bruckner with a sniff, as she appraised his physique.

"No, a fruit compote and coffee."

"No wonder you're so skinny."

Sage instantly knew he was never going to win around her, so he changed the subject. "Mr. Mills said I could have access to the big office and the balcony off the kids' bedrooms. I'll be doing some measuring and drawing. I'll probably be up there most of the day."

"Do whatever you need to do. Mr. Brand is not here today and Mr. Mills will not bring the mail until afternoon. Go down that hall and it will take you to the dining room off the entry."

Sage headed down the hall. He could feel he was still being watched until he passed through a swinging door into a formal dining room. He could see the staircase through the French doors.

The double doors to the big office were open. Sage had to fumble around for the light switch, since there was no natural light in the room, if Brand's small office door was closed. Inside the door, to the right, was a bank of switches. There was an ornate chandelier in the middle of the room in front of the large fireplace. There were also wall sconces on both sides of the fireplace above the mantel.

Sage immediately saw a problem. The crystals on the main lighting fixture cast little sparkles on the wall where he was going to paint. He couldn't have a little shiny spot on a hillside hundreds of yards away. That lighting fixture would have to go.

Also, about six feet high there was a thin molding about an inch wide that ran from wall too wall. In the center of the room, a vertical piece ran from the horrizonal to the floor.

The old photos were still splayed out on the table. He would go through them later, but the first order of business was to measure the wall and check for any idiosyncrasies that might present problems. From his case he pulled a large steel tape measure. The wall was twelve feet high. There was a cove molding, such as was in many of the elegant homes of the period. That would create no problems. Nor would the wide base molding complicate matters, since he was not painting a doorway where the floor had to be extended. The arched windows would be painted in, but he could preserve the structure at the top and at the bottom of the wall.

The wall was twenty-four feet long. The furniture was so massive and in such quantity that the room didn't appear to be that large. The new sheetrock had been covered with a very light texture before being painted the same light yellow as the rest of the room.

Sage sat for a time flipping through the various photos, reconciling angles, lighting, and all the other little jukes that photos can throw at a painter. He made note of all materials, textures, colors and flaws, including a nick in the marble sill. There may be a particular story behind that little blemish that his client might find endearing. Sage would have to check before painting that into the scene because it might also be the source of irritation concerning someone's stupidity, or it might bring back a bad memory.

Sage was about to adjourn to the balcony when Mrs. Bruckner popped into the room carrying a large tray laden with dishes and cutlery, announcing in a loud voice, "Lunch time."

That didn't correspond with his internal clock. Glancing at the grandfather clock in the corner, he noted it was just 11:00 o'clock.

Mrs. Bruckner caught him checking the time. "I know it's a bit early, but fruit doesn't last as long as a proper breakfast of a good porridge or ham and eggs." At the head end of the great table she began spreading a small white cloth, onto which she place a steaming soup bowl and ancillary plates. "Come, come, come, eat before it gets cold."

Sage was not in the habit of taking a large lunch. He was thinking hard on how to get out of the situation without offending Mrs. Bruckner, when he got a whiff of her offering. Sage wasn't much of a cook, but he was an accomplished eater.

"Why, Mrs. Bruckner, how kind of you. I usually don't worry too much about lunch...."

"I can see that," said the cook as she raised an eyebrow, again appraising his frame. Deflecting blame, she said, "What would Mr. Brand think of me if I let a guest in his house go hungry?"

Sage eyed a bowl of thick lentil soup with humped-up chunks of oxtail. The tantalizing smell of fresh-made bread escaped from a folded napkin in a basket. A container with butter and a knife were next to the basket. A thermal carafe of coffee with attendant containers of cream and sugar finished the setup. As Sage slid into the chairman's chair, Mrs. Bruckner handed him a cloth napkin. She waited long enough to see him start eating. "Leave the dishes there. I'll pick them up on my next rounds."

Although, he knew better, he continued eating until he was stuffed. The hot dark bread, dripping with butter, was too good to put down. Sage groaned as he got up from the table. He carried the carafe of coffee and a cup out onto the balcony where he began his sketches. It was almost four when his concentration was broken by Bert coming through Elke's room to join him in the afternoon sun.

"Are you getting what you need?" asked Bert as he took the other chair at the table.

"Yes, everything is going beautifully. I will have the sketch and the estimate ready by tomorrow morning."

"Mr. Brand will return this evening. He can see you at 10:00 in the morning, if that would be convenient."

"Perfect." Sage eyed Bert. "How do you and Mr. Brand keep from weighing 300 lbs with Mrs. Bruckner lurking in the kitchen?"

Bert laughed. "I warned you that being young and skinny was

a hazard around her. She's an interesting person."

"German?"

"Yes. Mr. Brand is Austrian. He hired her because she spoke German. He wanted to stay in touch with the language and he hoped some German would rub off on the kids. An American GI brought her back from Germany and then left her with a couple of boys. Both of them died young. She still thinks young men are all appetites. Mr. Brand and I are outside of her range because we are too old and, besides, I have a wife and it is her job to keep me properly fed. Anna wouldn't dare interfere with the duties of another woman."

*****

Promptly at 10:00 am, Sage was let in the back door by Mrs. Bruckner. Bert ushered him up to the upper office, where Mr. Brand was waiting at his large desk. After shaking hands, Sage laid out the sketch and also his bid for doing the job.

Mr. Brand studied the drawing minutely. Periodically, he would look at the end wall with a faraway look as if remembering what it was like before civilization moved in. Finally, he put the sketch to the side with the comment, "I like it."

Before Brand picked up the estimate, Sage said, "One point, something will have to be done about the crystal chandelier. You can't have those little specks of light striking the hillsides or it will ruin the entire image."

"Good thought. I can have that changed out. I have no particular emotional involvement with that thing. I always thought it was a little much, but my wife liked to see it from our room at the other end of the hall.

"Another item. May I remove that molding an fill behind it?"

"No. You will just have to live with that. Can you do so?"

"Certainly."

When Brand picked up the financial agreement, Sage said, "You will note there is an allowance for the accommodations on site as per Mr. Mills."

"Right." Brand carefully went through the legalese on the paper. "How long do you think the job will take?"

"Three to four weeks, providing nothing extraordinary happens."

"Such as?"

"Once there was a kitchen fire that smoked up the whole house. I couldn't get in for a week and then I had to clean everything and repaint some things."

"That is what clause eight is about?"

"Yes."

"When can you start?"

"I'll return home and make the full size cartoon. To get my equipment here, I'll be driving. I can start in ten days, if that would be convenient."

Brand looked at his calendar. "I won't be here for the first few days. Bert or Mrs. Bruckner can take care of things. Good." Brand picked up a pen and signed the contract.

"Bert will give you the down payment check. Leave my copy of the contract and a photocopy of the sketch with him. Thank you, Mr. Grayling. I am looking forward to seeing something besides a blank wall when I look west."

Chapter 3

Sage caught the next available flight back to Albuquerque. By the time he retrieved his van and drove home, it was dark. He let himself into the house and made the customary circuit, checking to see everything was all right. Satisfied that no disaster had taken place during his absence, he stripped off his traveling clothes and headed for the shower. After he had ritualistically ridded himself of the stink and grime of the city, he padded to the wet bar in his bedroom for a margarita made with Cointreau instead of Triple Sec. Sampling the salted rim with the tip of his tongue, Sage headed for the studio to get some busy-work done before calling it a day.

The studio took up the entire north end of the building. Originally, there had been two large bedrooms facing the garden. Since most of the brick roofs had either collapsed or were about to, Sage had knocked out all the interior dividing walls and had replaced their load-bearing functions with six-inch well casings. Strong-backs topped the steel columns to hold up the roof beams. The result was sixty feet of open space. Then he had removed the walls to a bedroom on the front and another on the back, which added another forty feet to the length of his studio, resulting in an open area of 20x100 feet.

Along the outer wall of the rear of the studio, he had built a section of drywall....two sheets tall and eight wide for a smooth surface measuring 16x32 feet. There was still almost two feet left to the ceiling. From roll ends of newsprint that he had scrounged from the local newspaper, he now started covering the wall with enough strips of paper to make the cartoon for the proposed painting. To work on the higher sections, he had constructed an easily moveable ladder and adjustable platform on balloon tires.

Sage was just finishing tacking the paper in place when he heard the blast of the ballsy truck horn. He hadn't had much time to think about the blonde potter. He stopped to listen to find out which way she was going. He also glanced around to make sure the window shutters were closed, since he wasn't wearing anything. The truck passed on by, heading for the highway. Tinna was working late. He readied everything for a clean start the next day.

Mornings were not one of Sage's best times. During his early aimless meanderings about the house, Tinna honked her way in. After his third cup of coffee, he was finally ready to tackle the enlargement of his sketch to actual size. He created a grid on the drawing he'd brought back from LA. Then he computed the enlargement factor and built a grid on the wallpaper by snapping chalk lines. It was nearly noon by the time he was satisfied with the results of his efforts.

Before trying to figure out what he had in the freezer for lunch, he decided to check on Tinna's progress. He pulled on a pair of pants and a T-shirt. Sticking his feet in a worn pair of moccasins and donning his "I Don't Do Mornings" baseball cap, he was ready to meet the world.

Considerable change had been wrought in his back acreage in the few days since the Icelandic potter had moved in. She had set up shop on the right edge of the cleared area where the bank was four or five feet high. The old-time flatbed Chevy was backed up to a large pile of cow chips. A blue tarp was thrown back. Apparently Tinna had dumped a new load of fuel. Forty feet off to the side was another tarp enclosing what Sage suspected to be a latrine. Tinna was not in sight, but occasionally he could hear a muttered oath coming from the other side of the truck.

Rounding the truck he came upon a view that made the trek from the house worthy of the effort. A tightly stretched pair of jeans, constraining a shapely posterior, protrudied from a little cave. The owner of the visage was on her knees digging like a badger. Dirt was flying out beside her legs and between her thighs. Sage waited a bit before thumping the door of the truck and yelling "Ahoy, the ship."

Tinna started. The reaction was followed by a long line of muted, unintelligible mutterings, which Sage took to be curses. The picturesque ass wriggled its way out of its earthly confines revealing a sweaty, dirt-covered irritated female, rubbing the back of her head.

"You," said Tinna accusingly.

"Were you expecting someone else?"

"No, I wasn't expecting anyone....at all"

"Sorry I startled you. Next time, I'll just pat you on the ass to let you know you have company," said Sage with a broad grin.

"Pendejo," said Tinna as she tried to dust herself off. All she accomplished was to make mud. She had been sweating profusely and the dirt made her look like a local native instead of a fair-skinned Icelander. The bandana she had tied around her head formed a dike to hold dirt. She was wearing a sports bra and low cut jeans over cowboy boots. Everything was filthy.

Tinna suddenly became self-conscious. Sage had already gotten the impression she was fastidious about her appearance and personal hygiene.

As Tinna was trying to get herself in a more presentable condition, Sage bent over to look into the cave. "Come winter, you'll probably find a bear in here. How much further in will you be going?"

"On this one....only about three feet more. I will be enlarging the interior to make a firing chamber. I still have to make a chimney. This one is just to run some experiments. I'm making some smaller pieces for a test firing. How did your trip to LA turn out?"

"Fine. I got the commission and possibly another in Texas. I'm doing the cartoon now and I'll drive to LA in a week. It's getting on toward lunch time. I was about to nuke one of those gourmet frozen dinners. Would you care to join me?"

"Oh, I can't. I'm in no shape to be seen in public." Tinna was still trying, with little success, to scrape off the mud.

"Before you dig much further, I'd think about shoring up the roof like the miners do. I'd hate to come out here and find only a pair of cowboy boots sticking out of a pile of dirt. I have no idea how stable that bank is."

Tinna was about to come back with some wise comment but thought better of it. She studied the cave for a moment before saying, "You're probably right. I had only planned on making a small kiln. I hadn't figured such a small one could be any hazard, but there is a lot of weight stacked above it."

"There's a pile of 4x4s in the thicket beside the garage. I used them while we were rebuilding the roofs. They're splattered with concrete, but they'll work for posts and top rails. You'll need something to form a roof. Those timbers are expendable....for a good cause. You can leave them in and they'll become fuel.... unless you want to be a purist and use only scheiße." Sage chuckled at his own funny.

His attempt at humor was rewarded with a sour look from the potter. Suddenly, she grabbed her right thigh and began clawing at it frantically.

"What's the matter?" said Sage.

"I just got bit by your mother," cried Tinna in reply. She broke into a self-satisfied grin as she waited for the next round.

Since Sage couldn't think of an immediate response appropriate to give a female, he shook his head and said, "Come over to the Lair. You can wash off that mud. If you're afraid of catching athlete's foot, you can use the shower on the far left. I use the one on the right."

Now, faced with the challenge of being afraid, Tinna fell in step with Sage as he headed back.

"All those forms in the shed are completely rotten. Would it be all right if I cleared them out so I could have somewhere to store tools and equipment?"

"Fine," said Sage. "But there's no roof."

"That's all right. Most of the stuff can be out in the weather. If not, I can put a tarp over it. I'll put a door on the shed so those tools don't walk off in the middle of the night."

As they passed through the granary, Sage pointed out a radial arm saw mounted along the rear wall. "You can use that saw to cut those 4x4s, providing you scrape off any concrete along the cut before running them through the blade."

"Thanks, that'll be a big help." Tinna was surveying the room. She'd passed through the room on her first visit, but then other things had commanded her attention. Now she had a chance to take in the entire facility. It was probably close to sixty feet long and forty feet wide. The ceiling was domed, giving the middle of the room around twenty feet clearance. There were no exterior windows, but there were four windows facing the walled-in garden area.

"Wow, what a space. It's as big as a shopping mall."

"Well, not quite. It's been a great workshop for doing the heavy construction in the house. I used to line up the forms for the ceiling beams on both sides and back a concrete truck down the middle pouring in both directions."

Instead of entering the kitchen via the pantry, Sage jogged left through the passage that led to the central jardin. Pointing to the first door on the left he said, "The showers are in there. There are towels in the ropero in the corner. There's soap and shampoo too. Come to the kitchen when you're finished. I'll have the coffee made."

Since he had time, he put a pot of real coffee on to brew. Ten minutes later, a funny sight appeared in the doorway. Tinna had her hair done up in a towel and a beach towel was wrapped around under her arms. With her height, it was provocatively short. Cowboy boots completed the outfit.

"Sorry, but those clothes were hopeless. When I spotted your drier in the corner, I washed me and them. What a muddy mess. I hope it doesn't clog up your drains."

"Oh, they'll probably survive. Want anything in your coffee?"

"No."

"Take your pick and if you're hungry, pick two." There was an array of frozen meals spread across the counter top.

Tinna settled on the teriyaki steak. Sage chose beef bourguignon. He put one into each microwave.

That's some bathroom you have. Are you running a sex parlor here?"

Sage laughed. "That's only half of what there used to be. Someone had the bright idea of turning this building into a school. They carved up one of the bedrooms into a boys' and girls' bathroom and locker room of sorts. I incorporated one bath into my bedroom. I took out all the benches and clothes hooks. One of these days, I'll figure out something better. Originally, there were no doors. You just walked around that baffle wall one way or the other. I had to install a door. It got a little chilly showering in the winter. I left the four toilet stalls, shower heads, and the wash basins.

"How come there are no doors on the stalls?"

"That was the boys' side. The ruling philosophy was that if one gives boys privacy, they do nasty things."

Sage dropped a key on the table. "This is to the passage door in the granary. You'll have to be able to get to the saw. Just make sure the place is locked up when you're not around. I'd appreciate it if you'd keep an eye on the Lair while I'm gone. If anything happens....that I can do anything about....my cell number is on that paper under the magnet on the refrigerator door.

*****

Four days later, Sage was pulling away from his garage to head for LA, when Tinna came rumbling in with her flatbed. She pulled to a halt and leaned out her window.

"What is that?" she demanded.

"Are you making a crack about my transportation?"

"I'm not making any value judgment. I'm just trying to find out what it is."

"It's a 1982 Cadillac Seville "Elegante.""

"That's what it used to be, before you got creative."

"Well, I did a little remodeling. Because I have so much equipment to carry, I was driving that bouncy, old van, which tended to make for very uncomfortable, dreary trips. A widow lady I know had her deceased husband's Caddy, with 6700 miles on it...garaged for years. She couldn't find the gas cap, so she never drove the car. When I got it, I built the rack on the top."

"From the front bumper to the back bumper?"

"Sometimes I have to carry twenty-foot beams and long extension ladders. My big paintings are eighteen feet long," said Sage defensively. "Besides, it pisses off every Cadillac owner who sees 'Dreadnought'. She says, 'up yours'."

Tinna shook her head, dropped the gear shift into low, and as she ground her way forward, she shouted, "Have a good trip."

Chapter 4

—⚊ɯɯ⚊—

Sage had been on the job for two weeks. Things had settled down into a routine. Mrs. Bruckner was still trying to fatten him up. They had struck a compromise. He came down from his room at 9:00 each morning. If Mr. Brand was in residence, they would eat together in the breakfast room. If Sage was alone, he would perch on a stool in the kitchen and practice his German with Mrs. Bruckner.

Sage would eat eggs and bacon two days a week. Two more days he'd manage oatmeal with a little sausage thrown in. The remaining days he could eat his fruit without verbal opposition, which meant Mrs. Bruckner won.

Following breakfast, Sage would take a large thermal cup of coffee up to the painting room. If Mr. Brand was home, he'd take a look at the painting. He would smile and nod before burying himself in his small office. The boss never tried to interfere in the creative process, much to Sage's relief.

At 1:00 pm, Sage took a lunch break. That was when Bert usually arrived with the mail and any other deliveries that were needed. If Mr. Brand wasn't around, Bert would sit with Sage and chat. These exchanges usually took place in the kitchen so Mrs. Bruckner could become involved. It was obvious to Sage that there was a lot of mutual respect in the household.

He filled his day with his meticulous work while listening to language lessons on a headset. On this job, it was German because of the availability of Mrs. Bruckner. Sage worked until 6:00 pm every evening. That left him just enough time to clean up, change clothes, and get out of the house before Mrs. Bruckner set the night security system. Sage would routinely vary his menu, stopping at various ethnic or regional restaurants. Following dinner, he'd take in a movie or a cultural event. He usually let himself back into the house, past the alarm system, between eleven and midnight. He'd take one last look at his painting before retiring.

A singular unpleasantry marred the period. One night, as he drove into the yard, he could see lights coming from the master bedroom. The security system was off. A slightly disheveled Mrs. Bruckner was loading a tray with freshly prepared food.

"Am I late for breakfast?" said Sage.

"No, Miss Elke and friend are paying us a visit. She usually appears when her father is out of town." A slight trace of disfavor showed through the usually proper front displayed by a servant toward an employer's offspring.

"Does she know I am in the house?"

"Certainly by now she does. Hope you didn't leave anything valuable lying around."

"Let me carry that tray for you."

"No, I have to wait for the water to heat for the herbal tea. You go get situated and maybe the food will divert their attention."

Wondering what Mrs. Bruckner meant by her last remark, Sage quietly ascended to the second floor. He could hear sounds coming from the master bedroom. As usual, he went first to take a final look at his painting before turning in. The loud snap of the old wall switch must have been audible in the master bedroom because the master bedroom door swung open a moment later.

Sage stood looking at a two-foot peace sign smeared in the middle of his landscape. Sage froze in his tracks. Red fury flared, but he quickly moved to quench the immediate responses that flashed to the fore. He was in a client's house reacting to the actions of the client's child. He decided any of those impulse reactions would place him in jeopardy with either his client or the law.... neither of which were in his best interests.

He slowly turned to face the front of the house. A little, pinch-faced female with her hair wrapped in a bath towel was looking around the jamb.

"Elke, I don't think the man appreciates your artistic talents."

"I can understand that. Just look at what he paints," said someone back in the room.

The turban-headed female drew back as a straight-haired brunette stepped into view. Sage recognized her to be Elke from the family photos and paintings scattered about the house. However, she was no longer the svelte teenager usually portrayed. She was now decidedly pudgy. A lot of unhealthy fat was visible around the pair of dirty, tattered jeans that she was clutching in front of her bosom. The pants hung down in front of her crotch. She was wearing only a pair of black bikini panties.

"Oh, he's a big one," said Elke as she swished out of the bedroom and around the staircase in what Sage could only guess was her interpretation of a provocative walk. All it did was make the fat jiggle. Under other circumstances, Sage would have laughed, but she looked like "trouble" on the prowl.

Elke advanced close enough that she had to look up at Sage. "I thought I made a vast improvement to that painting. No one has painted like that since they invented abstract art."

"Try improving my painting whenever you'd like. Each time, I'll charge your father an extra $1000. I'd say he is used to paying for your over-indulgences and idiocies."

"Chauvinist pig," screamed Elke, as she tried to rake his face with her right-hand fingernails.

Sage easily directed the swipe harmlessly off to the side.

Guessing that was only a faint, he was ready when she launched a right-footed kick at his groin. *Bitch.*

"Elke, behave yourself," cried Mrs. Bruckner, from the staircase.

Sage tucked in his left leg to protect himself. The barefoot blow glanced off his thigh. He grabbed the ankle in his left hand, holding it long enough to roll the interior of his thumb joint painfully along the tibia. That brought a loud cry of anguish. Sage flipped the foot upward causing a flailing of arms before she landed flat on her back on the floor. The jeans lost their strategic position, revealing pendulous breasts.

"Elke," said a stern Mrs. Bruckner. "I told you to behave yourself. You're indecent. Get to your room."

As Elke scrambled upright, Mrs. Bruckner and her huge tray of food were positioned between the two combatants. "Rouse, rouse." Using the tray as a battering ram, Mrs. Bruckner herded Elke back to her room. Miss Pinch-Face was apparently naked since she never exposed anything but her head around the door frame.

When Mrs. Bruckner kicked the door shut with a booming finality, Sage retreated to the painting room. The peace sign had been smeared on with one of his larger brushes using Viridian Green, one of the hardest colors on the palette to obscure. He couldn't afford to let the paint set up. He would have to deal with the mess immediately.

Before he touched anything, Sage went to his room for his digital camera. There were obvious signs that someone had been pawing around in his things. He had not removed the digital camera from one of the soft cases. The collapsed case, on the floor of the closet, looked empty. That is probably why Elke hadn't found the camera.

Sage recorded the entire painting scene, as well as the disarray in his bedroom before setting about the task of removing the sign from the wall. Armed with a roll of paper towels, a palette knife, a container of turpentine and a wastepaper basket to put it all in, he attacked the damage. He was still scraping off the thicker clumps when Mrs. Bruckner appeared.

"Oh dear, what are we going to do with her? Can you fix it?"

"Yes, it will just take time. The main problem is that it breaks my concentration. I had everything falling into place and now I have to detour. I must make this disappear before I can continue."

"Mr. Brand will be returning about noon tomorrow," said Mrs. Bruckner. "That means Elke will disappear before then."

Sage worked most of the night getting the last vestiges of viridian off the wall. The next morning he was a little late for breakfast. Mrs. Bruckner was tolerant of his tardiness, but she made him pay by serving him a heavy breakfast of bacon, potato pancakes and eggs.

At 9:00 am he had heard the girls vacating the master bedroom. They stayed away from him so there wasn't another confrontation. Bert put in an appearance at 11:00. He reported that he had dropped the girls off at the airport and they should be safely winging their way to Texas by then. Mrs. Bruckner had filled him in concerning the activities of the prior evening.

"I understand there'll be an additional $1000 charge to repair the damage. When you present your bill, give me a separate one covering that additional charge. I'll take it out of Elke's allowance." Bert smiled at the thought.

"How will Mr. Brand take news of last night's happening?"

"He'll be irritated....not at you. He spends a considerable amount of time and money cleaning up after his offspring. They were both good kids until they went off to college. The son became a party animal and Elke became a leftist, environmental activist....as long as she can cut holes in designer jeans to make herself look disgustingly impoverished. It is always easier to tolerate privation when one can slip off and refuel in a place like this."

Sage repaired Elke's damage. The painting progressed nicely. After another week, the end was in sight. Mr. Brand was in town on an important negotiation with the longshoremen's union over a project he had on the drawing board. Sage and Mr. Brand frequently ate breakfast together. Sage liked the developer. He seemed to be a straight shooter. His focus had switched from pure money making, since he already had more than he could ever spend, into investigating new concepts. The current project involved the development of one of the last remaining tracts of land suitable for large docking facilities. Brand's vision involved a new electronic system of moving and storing cargo around the port facility. The location of each piece could be accurately ascertained instantly. Such a novel installation was strongly opposed by the unions involved, on the basis that fewer people were needed to do a better, faster job.

One evening, as Sage cleaned brushes, he calculated he'd be finished with the painting by the weekend. There would have to be a drying time and then he'd return to apply the surface finish. He was already beginning to think of the project in Texas.

That evening he returned to the house about his normal time. The place was dark and silent. Sage let himself through the alarm system and went to the second floor. As usual, he stepped into the darkened room and flipped on the lights on the painting end of the room. He was pleased with the painting. He inhaled the pungent smell of paint and turpentine, which was one of his favorite fragrances. Mingled with the smells was a slight trace of something foreign that he couldn't immediately identify. Sage snapped off he lights and retired.

A high, piercing scream wrenched Sage out of a deep sleep. The screams continued gaining in volume. Sage rolled out of bed and headed for the door. The cries of distress were coming from the direction of his painting. Sage charged down the hall through the open double doors. It was early in the morning from the looks of the light filtering into the hallway. Mrs. Bruckner was standing in the doorway to Brand's small office screaming.

Sage grabbed her by the shoulders, saying, "What is it?"

As he said the words, his eyes told him. Brand was seated in his ergonomic chair with his head slumped forward on his chest. At the base of the skull was a black area with a trail of dark blood going down to his collar.

Sage was not all that familiar with dead bodies, but that looked like one to him. He swung Mrs. Bruckner around in the opposite direction ordering in German for her to be quiet. When he was sure she wouldn't fall, he let go of her and stepped to the side of Brand. Sage touched Brand's neck where the jaw sagged into it. The flesh was cold and unyielding. Sage stepped back and ran his artist's eyes around the room. Nothing seemed out of place from his meager knowledge of the room. Brand was dressed in his usual casual attire, slacks and open-throat sports shirt. However, he wasn't wearing the bone-colored street shoes he preferred, but was in a pair of slip-ons he wore around the house. The desk light was off, phone in the cradle, the recording machine off. There were two stacks of papers on either side of a single letter with an envelope stapled to it. The desk pen holder was empty. The pen was on the floor to the right of the body. There was a radio and TV in the room, but neither was on. From the position of the body, it appeared that Brand had been leaning back in his chair with the pen in his hand when he was shot.

Sage tested the air because he was smelling the same little odor that had twitched his curiosity the night before. It was stronger in the office and he identified it as gunpowder. The clock over the desk read, 7:15. He started to pick up the phone to make a 911 call, but thought better of it.

Mrs. Bruckner had stopped screaming. She was sobbing violently, hiding her head in her hands. Sage steered her to a chair at the large conference table and told her to sit while he called the authorities.

As he headed back to his room for his cell phone, he realized he was stark naked. He pulled on a pair of pants before dialing the phone. When the operator came on line, Sage said, "I am reporting a death. The deceased is Dieter Brand." He gave the address and answered a few questions as to who he was and the bare-bone circumstances. The operator was a little skeptical at first, since the phone showed up as a cell call and not from the address he gave. He ended the conversation by saying it didn't appear to him to be a natural death.

After the phone call, Sage turned his attentions to Mrs.

Bruckner. She was still sobbing as if her world had ended. He gently helped her to her feet and said, "Come, get me a cup of coffee before the police get here. You can wait in your room, instead of having to remain here. I'll take care of the authorities."

Sage helped her down the stairs and to the kitchen, where she began to regain function in the familiar setting. Sage knew the coffee had been made as soon as she got up. Mrs. Bruckner poured Sage a cup. "One for you, too," he said. The cook went through the motions mechanically.

They sat at the kitchen table. "We have a few minutes before anyone gets here. Tell me everything about this morning." He had to coax her some more. Ultimately he got her talking, but she was telling him in vernacular German, which was testing his knowledge of the language.

"I got up as usual, at 6:00. I came to the kitchen to start breakfast. Mr. Brand had an early meeting. When he didn't come down for breakfast, I went to remind him. I tapped at his bedroom door, but no answer. I thought he was in the office. I found him and I screamed."

"Did you turn on the alarm last night?"

"Yes."

"When?"

"At the usual time, 7:00."

"Was Mr. Brand here then?"

"Yes."

"Did he go out last night?'

"Not before I went to sleep."

"Did anyone visit him?"

"No."

"Did you hear anything strange in the night?"

"No."

"Did you hear me come in?"

"No. I am used to you now."

"Did you take the alarm off this morning?"

"Yes, when I came to the kitchen. The maids will be in today."

Sage was listening to sirens in the distance. "The police will be coming. I need to call Bert before they get here. What is his number?"

The cook reached to pick up the wall phone and pushed one the numbers in the memory. She handed the phone to Sage.

Mrs. Mills answered the call.

"Hi, this is Sage Grayling, the painter. I need to talk to Bert."

"He's in the shower."

"Get him out. This is urgent."

A few moments later, Bert came on the line. "Sage?"

"Yes. You'd better get over here as quickly as possible. Mrs. Bruckner found Brand in his office with what I believe is a bullet hole in the back of his head. He's been dead for some hours. The police are a few blocks away."

"I'll be there shortly." Bert hung up.

Sage rushed upstairs to his bedroom to get his digital camera. He quickly made a pictorial record of the little office and the outer office. When he heard the siren he put his camera away and returned to the kitchen where he refilled his coffee cup before heading for the front door to let the police in. As he stepped out onto the porch, a marked Sheriff's Office car pulled up under the portico. A very young looking deputy stepped out of the car. He straightened his uniform as he strutted around the car and in a rather officious manner stated, "You found a body."

Sage let the deputy get close enough so he could look down on him. When Sage didn't immediately answer, the deputy said, "Are you going to answer me?"

"Answer what? You haven't asked a question." *You arrogant asshole.*

"Don't be cute. You know what I mean."

"I know what you say, but I may not know what you mean."

Sage knew he was just making the situation worse, but he detested little Napoleons behind badges. To return to the real problem, he amended his attitude and said, "If you want to see the body, follow me." Sage was still only wearing a pair of paint-smeared pants. He wheeled about on a bare heel and led the way up the stairs to the office. He stepped aside at the private office door so the deputy could see Brand slumped over in his chair. Apparently the deputy came to the same conclusion as Sage that they were looking at a bullet hole at the base of the skull.

Huxley, from the name on his chest tag, stepped in front of Sage and tried to back him out of the entry to the room. When they bumped chests, Huxley said, "Out. This is a crime scene now. Sit down at that table."

Sage retreated to the chair where Mrs. Bruckner had sat a few minutes earlier. He took a drink of coffee as the deputy called the office on his portable radio. Huxley stepped far enough to the side to be out of sight. He was trying to keep his voice low, but Sage could still pick up snatches. The captain was to be called. There were comments about lots of money, big time hit, and newspapers.

While waiting for backup, Huxley drew up a chair across the table and began prodding Sage for information. Sage said he was the painter doing that piece at the end of the room. He was staying in a room down the hall. Sage related that he had been awakened by the cook, Mrs. Bruckner, who had screamed when she discovered the body.

Another patrol car arrived outside. Huxley started for the door and then thought better of leaving Sage alone at a crime scene, so he directed Sage to let the others in. This time there were two more uniformed deputies. A pair of two plainclothes detectives arrived next. By then, there were enough officers hanging around, he didn't have to run their errands. Sage remained sitting at the conference table as various other officials asked him questions. He directed one of the detectives to Mrs. Bruckner, who was waiting in the kitchen. The forensic team arrived to begin taking photos and spreading black powder all over creation.

The other detective sat down across from Sage and introduced himself as Lieutenant James B. Fuente.

"Is that Jaime B. Fuente or James B. Fountain?"

"Oh, you speak Spanish," said the lieutenant with just the faintest twitch of a smile.

"No, not really. I know this is a serious business, but everyone is so grim. I hope that whatever you guys have isn't contagious."

Fuente hesitated a moment before saying, "Not to outsiders." He then reestablished his role of inquisitor. Sage went through all the material that Huxley had covered before delving into information concerning Brand. Sage gave any facts he had concerning name, marital status, relatives, but deferred to either Mrs. Buckner or Bert on personal matters.

Considerable time was spent as to Sage's movements, particularly when it related to the alarm system, once Sage had mentioned that there was one. Fuente made Sage minutely account for his entire evening. He inquired as to anything Sage may have seen or heard that was out of the ordinary.

"Brand was killed before I got home last night."

"And what makes you think that?"

"After I got home, I checked on my painting before going to bed. I detected a faint odor, which I couldn't place at the moment, but when I entered Brand's office after Mrs. Bruckner found him, the odor was more concentrated. It was gunpowder."

"And how is it that you recognize the smell of gunpowder?" said Fuente.

"I gave you my address as a rural route in Albuquerque, New Mexico. The chances are that anyone with such an address would recognize gunpowder. Besides, I do a lot of rodent plunking at my place."

The sounds of an argument wafted up the stairs. Sage recognized Huxley's voice shouting down Bert. Sage turned to Fuente. "If you want to get any information concerning the victim, you'd better shut that little shit up, before he pisses off the best source of information you've got. That's Bert Mills, Brand's right-hand man."

"Sit tight," said Fuente as he bounded toward the door. He was yelling Huxley's name before he got to the staircase.

The argument ceased abruptly. Sage sat with his empty coffee cup, wondering if he could slip off to get dressed and get a refill. He decided against it when he heard a shout from below, "The sheriff's here." The word was passed by someone in the upper hall to the office. Everyone suddenly got a ramrod up their ass and became ultra-efficient.

A few minutes later, a tall, distinguished man with steel-grey hair worn in a tight, wavy close crop, came striding into the room. He was dressed in an immaculate, tailored uniform. One of the deputies met him and indicated the proper direction with a sweep of the hand. The sheriff stopped in the small office doorway to survey the scene. Brand had not been moved yet. One of the sheriff's minions gave him a briefing on what had been found.

The sheriff grunted and stepped out of the small office. "Who's that?" he demanded, flicking his riding crop toward Sage.

"He's the artist doing that painting at the end of the room."

The sheriff glanced at the painting and the laid out painting materials. Then he looked up and down Sage's bare torso. "What's that poof doing in the middle of a crime scene? Get him down to the dining room with the rest of the people."

Sage slowly got up. He was sure he'd just been insulted or slandered but he didn't quite know the extent of it. He went out into the hall and headed for his bedroom.

"Where are you going? I said the dining room," shouted the sheriff in a big, bull voice that could have been heard by the dolphins off the coast.

"To my bedroom. I'm going to get dressed before appearing in public."

"This whole floor is a crime scene."

"Not my clothes. I'm either going to get dressed or I'll tell the evening news you like my body so much that you wouldn't let me get dressed," shouted Sage loud enough to be heard throughout the house.

The sheriff puffed up and turned red in the face. He was about to come back with something which would not be designed for Sage's comfort or benefit but ended up growling, "What are you doing here, Webster?"

Coming up the stairs, in the company of Lieutenant Fuente, was a set of jowls. As the jowls advanced they topped a portly figure dressed in a designer suit. "I received a report that you have a high profile case. It's the District Attorney's job to keep you from getting into trouble. It sounds as if I arrived just in time."

The DA looked Sage up and down. "There's a hot, little reporterette in the front that would love to interview you just as you are. She's setting up with the TV truck outside the gate. Their camera already has a view of the entire front of the house."

"Fuente, go with him to change clothes. Seize and tag the clothes he wore last night. Make sure he doesn't destroy anything. Don't let him back on this floor."

"Yes, sir."

Fuente nodded his head in the direction of the bedroom. As the lieutenant closed the door, he glanced back to made sure the sheriff was occupied. "It's not good to cross him. He has plenty of power and a long memory."

"What does "Poof" mean?"

Fuente hesitated for a moment before saying, "It's our dear leader's code word for queer, homo, gay, or effeminate. I think it's a term used in England. Anyway, he started using it after a conference he attended in London. That way he doesn't have to use those politically charged words. Why?"

"That's what he called me."

"You're an artist. In his world, all artists are queer."

"He's not the only one with a long memory." Sage stripped of his paint pants. "Do I have time for a shower and shave?"

"Don't push it."

"Okay, the clothes on the chair are the ones I wore last night."

"Shoes and socks?"

Sage rolled his eyes. "Beside the bed." Sage got a fresh set of clothes. Fortunately, he'd emptied his pockets the night before and the contents were on the dresser. He scooped his billfold and car keys into his pockets. He also palmed his camera.

When Sage was dressed, Fuente escorted him to the dining room. Bert was occupied with a detective in his little office off the entry. Another detective was at the dining table with Mrs. Bruckner. He was looked completely exasperated. When Sage entered the room, Mrs. Bruckner burst into tears again and started wailing in German, asking what was going to happen. She said the police terrified her. She declared she didn't know anything. She didn't know anyone who would want to hurt Mr. Brand.

Sage went to the terrified woman and put his arms around her telling her in German that this terrible thing would be over soon. The police had to get information and then they would go away.

"So you speak German. I need you to translate for me. I can't seem to get through to her."

Sage pulled out a chair next to Mrs. Bruckner. "Now Anna let me help you get through this thing. If we are going to find out who did this, the police need information. If you can't find the words, I'll translate. First, let's all go into the kitchen and get some coffee."

Turning to the detective, Sage said, "This lady is a servant in this household. She doesn't think she should be sitting at this table. Let's go into her domain, the kitchen, and everything will go much smoother."

Without waiting for an answer, Sage helped the cook to her feet and moved toward the kitchen.

Once Mrs. Bruckner was in the kitchen, she calmed down considerably. She poured three mugs of coffee and set up the service. At the counter, where Sage ate breakfast and chatted with the cook, the detective resumed his interview. In the more familiar surroundings and with Sage's accompaniment, she regained some of her English. Sage helped her over the tough spots. Then, the questioning took a turn that frightened Mrs. Bruckner and disgusted Sage. The detective was trying to establish some relationship between the servant and some outside entity who bought his way into the house to kill Brand. There were intimations of money transferring hands. There were questions about her belonging to social societies or unions. He tried to delve into her financial standing.

At that point, Sage said in German, "Anna, you've given all the information that is needed. Don't say anything more until you have talked to Bert. Tell him the kind of questions the police are asking and have him get an attorney to advise you."

Turning to the detective, Sage asked, "What is your name?"

"Why?"

"You are getting absolutely insulting with your line of questioning. I have advised Mrs. Bruckner to not answer any further questions until she has consulted with an attorney. She must be able to tell her attorney who has been acting so improperly."

The detective sat there saying nothing.

"Must I go to the sheriff to find out who you are?"

As Sage suspected from what he had seen, the deputies were afraid of their boss. "I'm Sergeant Robert Tinker. Hey, don't get jumpy. We have to ask these kinds of questions. Right now we have three suspects, you two and that guy out front with Myers. Only you three have the new security code. Your boss has been hit by what looks like a professional hit man. He had to get in here somehow. Someone helped him or he diddled the system. So we ask questions."

"You're asking the wrong people," said Sage with emphasis.

A uniformed officer stuck his head in the kitchen. "I've got two women who say they are cleaning maids waiting to get in. What do you want to do with them?"

Tinker turned to Mrs. Bruckner. "Who are they?"

The cook was back to speaking German. Sage translated. "Two women come in once a week to do the heavy cleaning. This is their day."

"Put them in the dining room. Someone will talk to them," said Tinker. "Has the sheriff left yet?"

"No, he's out getting face time with the press," said the officer.

Tinker growled. "Watch your mouth." He shot Sage a sideways glance.

Sage had caught the whole byplay. *Fear and respect are incompatible,* thought Sage.

It turned into a long, tedious day. At least Sage and Mrs. Bruckner were able to stay in the kitchen during the proceeding. Periodically, one of the officials came to question them on some aspect of the routine. By noon, Bert was able to join them. Sage put Mrs. Bruckner to work getting soup and sandwiches for the three of them. She also made a coffee service for the dining room for the deputies and a flock of assistant DAs, who had arrived.

Sage and Bert compared notes quietly as the cook moved about the kitchen. She did not seem inclined to want to overhear their conversation. She banged kettles and plates around so as not to be able to hear.

Bert said he had given the detective all the pertinent information concerning Brand and his family. The deputies wanted to check on the locations of the two kids to see if they could have committed the murder. It had tentatively been determined that the cause of death was a small caliber gunshot through the brain stem into the skull.

"Where are the kids?" said Sage.

"As far as I know Karl is still in Rio. Elke said she was going to the house in Texas when she left here the other day."

"Who's notifying them?"

"I was going to try as soon as I got here, but the detectives wouldn't let me. This is a big enough story that the kids will find out over TV, if they are anywhere near a set. If they don't hear it themselves, some friend will undoubtedly tell them. Unfortunately, this will not be completely unwanted news for them. Both are panting for a chance to spend dad's money. However, I don't think they will be entirely pleased with how things are set up."

Sage raised his eyebrows, but didn't inquire further. It wasn't his problem. "That detective Tinker said the three of us are suspects because we have the code to the house. Don't the kids?"

"No. Recently, Mr. Brand changed the codes to keep them out. Elke steals anything of value and misuses everything else. He didn't want her to have free access to the place. If Karl could get in, he'd have 500 people in for a big blast....all on dad's tab. Besides, I called the security company and their records show only three activations....when Mrs. Bruckner set it at 7:03, your return at 11:32 and Mrs. Bruckner turning the system off at 6:13 this morning."

"Is there any way of getting into the house without going through the system?"

"All the doors and windows are wired. Detective Fuente is outside with the gardeners going over the entire outside of the house to see if anything is amiss. I suppose an expert could bypass the system, but I don't know anything about that."

Sage brought up a subject closer to home for him. "What about my painting. Where do I stand?"

"Soon as they will let you back in, finish the painting and I'll pay the rest of the bill. It can't be left as it is. Also proceed with the one in Texas. I'll call Luke Halliday, my business twin in Dallas, to set it up. The houses will probably be sold and the paintings will be necessary to make them more saleable."

Sage was greatly relieved to know he was going to get paid. He had already earmarked that money for certain upcoming bills and future projects.

Their conversation was interrupted by Mrs. Bruckner serving thick lentil soup and Braunschweiger sandwiches made of heavy, dark bread. Neither man had had breakfast and the repast was well received. Mrs. Bruckner refused to join them, preferring to sit by herself at a side counter.

The afternoon passed slowly. Bert was continually digging up information for the detectives. Of particular interest to the investigators were matters pertaining to the pending deal for the cargo handling facility. Brand had been locked in a dispute with the longshoreman's union boss, Tony Roskal. The newspapers had been making a big play of the battle between the futurist developer and the entrenched unions and the whispered backing of organized crime that controlled them. As it was playing out, there was financing waiting in the wings and the project was moving toward reality despite all the threats and delaying tactics. The detectives wanted dates and times of meetings between the factions, names of those involved, notes concerning the discussions and agreements. Outside of pure calendar notations, Bert drew the line. If they wanted more confidential information, they would have to go through the corporate attorneys.

After a particularly combative session with an assistant DA, Bert locked the safe, his file cabinets and his office door and stomped off to the kitchen, where he called Brand's attorney and suggested that he get an immediate injunction to keep the sheriff and the DA out of Brand's files. Bert maintained they were on a fishing expedition trying to get any adverse information on the union, Roskal, or any political opponents whose names might appear.

Second floor activities were winding down. Brand's body had been removed. The forensic team had departed. All the minor characters such as the gardeners and maids had long since been sent out. Lieutenant Fuente came into the kitchen with instructions.

"This house is being designated as a crime scene until the sheriff wants to lift the restriction. Since Mrs. Bruckner lives here, she can stay in her rooms and the kitchen, but she is not to enter the rest of the house. There will be a deputy stationed inside and one will be outside. No one else is allowed in.

"Mr. Mills, you may leave now, but keep yourself available in case you are needed.

"Mr. Grayling, you are to leave now."

"My clothes and property are upstairs."

"That will all have to stay here until the restriction is lifted," said the detective.

"And how long will that be?"

"I have no idea. It depends on how the case progresses. It could be a few days, a week or a year. The sheriff will make that decision. Oh, yes, that Caddy outside is yours, right?"

"Yes."

"Give me the key. It is being impounded. It will be released by forensics if they find it to be clean."

"What?" demanded Sage in disbelief.

"Give me the keys or we'll have to break into it. A tow truck is on the way. And let us know where you are staying, in case we need to talk to you further."

"If I hadn't insisted on getting dressed this morning, I suppose he'd have kicked me out into the mountains, miles from any commercial area with only a pair of pants and bare feet."

"I told you, it's not in your best interests to cross the sheriff."

"Bastard!" *I'll have to turn a little creative thought in his direction.*

Fuente shrugged and held out his hand. Standing at his full height, Sage towered over the detective, who was even more intimidated when he looked up at the artist's thin lips and narrowed eyes. As the detective took the keys, he said, "Join the crowd."

So Fuente thinks he's a bastard too.

"I'll put you up for the night at my place," said Bert.

"If you'll take me into Santa Monica and drop me off at a decent motel, I'll take it from there."

Chapter 5

—〰—

Sage checked into a motel on the coast highway, not too far from where Bert lived. He immediately arranged for a rental car and then headed for the motel bar for a martini. The TV was showing the local news. The lead story was the murder of a prominent LA real estate developer. It was being characterized as a possible gangland hit because of the nature of the death and the deceased's involvement as an adversary of local crime syndicates. Then Sheriff Harvey L. Swain was shown giving a press interview with the Brand house in the background. Sage knew much more than the sheriff was saying, but what he was listening to was the way in which the sheriff was saying it.

He's a frigin' politician. He's on the make for something bigger. Brand's death is just a stepping stone.

Sage limited himself to one martini for a couple of reasons. He couldn't take any more of that slop over the television and he had to go shopping for necessities. The motel directed him to a nearby mall where he was able to pick up an emergency pack of clothes and toiletries. He had a late dinner at the motel, another martini and then headed for his room. He didn't even turn on the TV but lay back on the bed trying to make some sense out of the day's happenings. Since he hadn't killed Brand and he was pretty sure neither Mrs. Bruckner nor Bert had done the deed and the police had eliminated both the kids, Sage was out of possible suspects. Of course, the murder wasn't his concern. His only problem seemed to be the sheriff. That slimy politician was costing him a bundle of money. Lost time on the job was the biggest expense. Add to that the motel, car rental and the various other ancillary expenditures, and it would eventually amount to a considerable sum.

The next morning, Sage had breakfast before calling Bert to see if there had been any developments. Bert knew of none. He was going to the post office and would be back in twenty minutes. He suggested Sage come over to the house so they could talk.

Sage found the house without difficulty. He was rather surprised at how modest it was when one considered that Bert's services had been so vital to such a wealthy man. Surely, the salary for such responsibility would be substantial.

Mrs. Mills answered the door and directed Sage off into the bedroom wing. Bert was seated at a slab door propped up on small filing cabinets to make a big table. On his left was a big stack of identical envelopes. Bert was slicing open the envelopes, extracting a check from each and putting it on a stack to the right.

"You'll have to sit on the bed until I get finished. This is my son's room. He's off to college, so I use the space for busy-work. These are the monthly rent checks from the phone company. They design the buildings they want, Brand builds them and the company leases them. It tends to be good, long-term business after they install millions of dollars of equipment in a building. They can only write $5000 checks without jumping through hoops, so we get multiples of $5000."

"I watched Sheriff Swain on TV last night. He's not a lawman, he's a politician. What's he gunning for?"

"Although neither will admit it, both he and the DA are gunning for a run at the governor's job the next time around."

"That's why sparks were flying at the house yesterday when

Webster arrived."

"Dieter's murder is big news around here. There will be a lot of mileage gained if Swain can catch the murderer and Webster can successfully prosecute him. Both will be squeezing the case for every bit of publicity that it's worth."

"What's going to happen to you with your boss dead?"

"I'm going to miss Dieter like hell, because we were very good friends, but my job won't change too much. Dieter knew that neither of his kids could ever handle the business, so he didn't give it to them. They don't know this yet, but a trust was set up. I'll run the California trust. For years, he and his wife were involved in many charitable endeavors. When Helga died, he formalized a lot of endowments in her name. The business will continue to fund the various charitable efforts."

"I don't suppose that is going to make his heirs very happy. Won't they spend the rest of their lives challenging the will?"

"Dieter figured they probably would try, but he's got things pretty well locked down. Oh, his offspring won't be wanting. They will each come into a chunk of money. When they were born, Dieter gave them the maximum allowable tax-free gift. They got a like amount on every birthday. As soon as the money was given, Pop borrowed it back at the maximum allowable interest. Compounded, that represents a tidy sum. They will get that right away and they will continue to get their monthly allowances, which are not too shabby. They won't be wanting.

"The one I'm worried about is Anna Bruckner. If the police get to snooping around too much they will probably find she is an alien. With all of the recent interest in illegal immigration, she might end up getting deported."

"She's been in this country a long time, hasn't she?" said Sage. "Didn't she take steps to become a citizen?"

"It's a strange, convoluted story. Anna met a GI stationed in Germany. They fell in love. For some reason they didn't get married over there. He returned home and later sent money for her to go to Mexico. She couldn't get into the states directly. He smuggled her across the border. She thought they were going to get married and it would all work out. However, it turned out that he was from a very strict Seventh Day Adventist family and when they found out about Anna, they laid down the law. He couldn't marry her. He did get away long enough to get her pregnant twice. And then he married a proper Adventist girl and disappeared, leaving Anna with two little boys. She never did try for citizenship. Anna's been hiding out in Dieter's kitchen for years."

"Have you got any ideas about who killed Brand?"

"Dieter had any number of business rivals, but with them it is always a game. This time I win and then next time you win. When Dieter won, it was fair and square. I don't know of anyone in the business community who could claim that he pulled a dirty deal on them."

"What about that Tony Roskal?"

"I can see why the authorities are looking in his direction. He has a tough-guy image. There have been all sorts of rumors floating around for years that he's ordered any number of hits. Dieter was winning the battle for the new port facility. Now, the deal will never be put together unless someone else does it.. I can't do it. I don't have Dieter's touch in such matters. I'll be managing what has already been done and if the phone company needs another facility, I'll get it up for them, but I won't be bringing in new concepts."

"How long do you think the house will be off limits?"

"I talked with Anna early this morning. There are officers all over the place. They still can't figure how the murderer got into the house—or out, for that matter. I'll bet it will be days before they will release the place."

"That bastard Swain will keep my car as long as possible just out of spite."

"That's a pretty good guess."

"Fuente said that I was supposed to let them know where I was staying....right?"

"That's what he said."

"Well, as soon as I get back to Albuquerque, I'll fax him my address and phone number in case he wishes to speak to me again. He can drop in any time he wants."

"Ooh, you like to live dangerously, don't you?"

"As soon as I can get back into the house, I'll finish the painting."

*****

Finally, Sage got a standby flight home. Again, he had to rent a car to get home. It was well after dark before he reached the Hacienda. Since he didn't have the door opener, he had to let himself into the garage with a key. When he made his rounds, he could see signs of Tinna having used the power saw in the granary and there was a pile of mail on the kitchen table.

Sage showered, mixed a martini and settled down in his bedroom office to check the mail. Most of it went into the trash can. Some went through the shredder. There was a blast from the ballsy horn. He paused to determine that Tinna was headed out. There was a ton of email, but it was almost all spam. There were a couple of inquiries concerning paintings from his website. Neither of them appeared to hold much promise. The answering machine did nothing to raise any hope for future projects.

As per request, Sage advised Detective Fuente of his whereabouts....by fax. He also added that he would be available any time Fuente wanted to drop in for a chat.

As he was turning out the lights, there was another horn blast from an inbound truck. Tinna must be tending a firing. Sage had an impulse to wander over to see what was happening, but he decided he didn't want to spend the rest of the night telling her about his boss being murdered. Besides, he wasn't feeling all that sociable. He was still smarting over having his Caddy impounded.

In the middle of the night, Sage was suddenly wide awake. Something had startled him but he didn't know what. He lay perfectly still listening. By turning his head slightly he could see the big, red digital numbers of the alarm clock. It was 3:30 in the morning. There were no night-lights in the house. It was close to a full moon, which, at that hour, was hanging behind the house. The bedroom side of the house was in darkness, but the courtyard and the portales on the front of the house were bathed in bright moonlight.

Sage wondered if Tinna had come into the granary for some reason. That noise would have aroused him. A slight shuffling sound came from direction of the living room. He wondered whether an animal had gotten into the house. One of the old, Mexican door latches had just been opened. It was either the one from the living room into the entry way or the one across the entry into the unfinished part of the studio along the front wall.

Quietly, Sage slid out of bed and padded to the window to look out into the jardin. There was a flicker of a flashlight coming from the entry. Sage followed the intruder's progress into the front studio, which was a vacant area 20 feet wide and 60 feet long. The last twenty feet was actually part of the hundred-foot long painting studio. Currently that space was being used just for storage. Through the windows into the jardin he could vaguely make out the shape of one figure, which he presumed to be a male. He was using a small, tight-beamed flashlight. Sage wondered how the intruder had gotten in. The front passage door had a very good Mexican lock. Mexicans know how to make locks. He doubted that was the source of entry. The intruder was being quiet, but he was not acting as if he expected anyone to be home. Of course, no one was supposed to be home. Sage hadn't been expected back for another week or two. And if Swain had had his way, Sage would be getting butt strain in a motel.

Sage let himself through the sliding glass door from his bedroom into the Great Studio, as he called it. He slipped over to the back wall and lifted a recurve hunting bow down from a hook. Stepping over to a floor rug, he used it to muffle any sound of the planted end of the bow as he stepped through to string it. Next to the wall was a concrete tile standing on end holding a handful of target arrows. Sage pulled out a couple. At the far end of the studio, a hundred feet away, were several bales of straw stacked up against the front wall giving Sage an indoor target range. Far enough to the right of the straw so a wild arrow wouldn't hit it, was an antique ropero, or freestanding closet. There was a lock on it because it housed his varmint rifles and ammunition, hunting arrows, knives and generally dangerous objects he didn't want lying around.

The intruder was focusing his attention on the ropero. Sage could hear metallic sounds as he played with the little padlock. Sage decided it was time to put a stop to the intrusion. He nocked an arrow and aimed for the left leg. The twang of the bow froze the intruder, but the impact of the arrow made him jerk. The arrow apparently penetrated the leg and went thunk into the ropero. There came a muted groan from the intruder, followed immediately by the discharge of a good-sized handgun. In the enclosed area of the studio the sound smacked off the walls. There was a cracking sound as the arrow shaft was broken and the figure disappeared back the way it had come.

The addition of a handgun complicated matters. Sage nocked another arrow, wishing he had the bladed hunting arrows instead of the target tips. He was slipping back into his room to get a better view of the courtyard when he heard the sound of the front door lock and the squall of the wrought-iron hinges. Sage slipped out of the bedroom into the portales, moving to the right to be able to see down the entryway. By the time he got into position, the door was standing open and there was no one to be seen.

Sage darted through the companionway and up the outside stairs to the roof. He moved to the front of the house where he had a good view of the moonlight-flooded landscape. Nothing was moving. A sound to his right rear attracted his attention. He ran back along the roof. Behind the garage he found a van had been pulled up along the back wall of the garage, which was slightly lower than the wall of the house. There was a stepladder leaning from the top of the truck to the top of the garage wall. The noise was from the intruder getting into the driver's door of the van. There was no attempt to cover the sound. He slammed the door. Sage dropped his bow and hefted an eight-foot, 4x4 from a stack. Using it like an oversized javelin, he launched it at the windshield. The timber smashed through the glass impaling itself into the driving compartment. The door swung open and the intruder fell out of the van onto the ground. He quickly gathered himself and hobbled around the van and disappeared. By the time Sage got to the front of the house, there was no visible motion. The quickest escape route would be into the brush beyond the side of the garage.

A chill ran down Sage's spine. Once in the brush, a turn to the right would lead him right back to where Tinna might be. He hadn't heard her leave, so the chances were good she was still tending her kiln. Sage raced down the stairs, slammed the front door as he headed for the ropero where he'd nailed the intruder. He snapped on the lights as he went by. The key to the lock was on top of the cabinet easily within reach of someone 6-foot-4. He opened the cabinet to retrieve his Winchester 218B. Though it was a good varmint gun, it was not especially good for man hunting, but that was the most firepower he could muster. He levered the chamber open to make sure it was loaded. He ran into his bedroom for a pair of shorts and moccasins. He remembered to grab his keys on the way out.

Sage let himself out the back door of the granary, making sure it was locked behind him. As quietly as possible he trotted back toward the brick yard while keeping his eyes open for the intruder. Tinna's truck was pulled up so the headlights could shine on the area. A warm glow was coming from the mouth of the cave. Tinna was not in sight.

Guessing she was snoozing in the truck, Sage rapped on the truck bed as he moved alongside while calling her name in a low voice. "Tinna, Tinna, Tinna." As he got to the door, he heard movement. A groggy, blonde head raised above the sill. Sage was standing in the glow of the kiln so she recognized him at once. He put his finger to his lips to indicate silence, hoping the sign was the same for Icelanders. Then he motioned for her to come out.

Tinna levered the door open. Sage said in soft voice. "There's a man with a gun out here." He swept his hand off in the direction the man had taken. "We've got to get to the house. Come."

Momentarily, she hesitated. A nearly naked man with a rifle was telling her to go to his house. But, she had no reasons to suspect he had any intention of hurting her, so she bailed out of the truck. She was fully dressed down to her cowboy boots.

Sage set out at a trot with Tinna right behind. Sage let them in the door and then dropped the bar that locked both the big and little doors. It would take a big truck to break through there. He led the way to the house where he checked the front door. He also dropped the bar there. The only other entry would be through the garage into the kitchen. That door was locked too.

"I have to check on one other thing," said Sage. He loped up onto the roof. The van looked unchanged. Sage dropped onto the garage roof and pulled the ladder up over the parapet.

He rejoined Tinna in the kitchen. "Put on some coffee water while I call the Sheriff's Office." On the 911 call he stated who and where he was and that he had just flushed an intruder. The guy had an arrow hole in his left leg. He was also armed with a large caliber handgun of some sort. He was afoot in the area since his van had been rendered inoperable.

As Tinna listened to the report, any reservations about Sage dissipated. She spooned Nescafe into the cups and impatiently waited for the water to boil. When Sage hung up she said, "Okay, what happened?"

"It'll take at least twenty minutes for a patrol car to get here unless one happens to be in the area. Pour the water and let's go see where I hit him."

Sage led the way into the studio area. Tinna had never seen that portion of the house. To the general public the place would have been a big, ugly barn of a place, but as an artist to whom space is golden, Tinna was highly impressed. She followed the painter through to the ropero. The arrow was in two pieces on the floor. Sage carefully inspected the face of the carved ropero. He found the hole where the small point of a target arrow had dented the wood. Measuring the hole against his leg and then compensating for height, Sage finally concluded, "It was pretty high in the thigh or in his butt. A little further to the right and I might have gotten his huevos."

Tinna looked blank.

"Huevos means eggs....another Mexican name for balls."

"Ha!" said Tinna with a laugh.

They followed a little trail of blood drops to the front door. "There isn't much a thief would want to steal around here, unless it would be kitchen appliances to hawk for a few bucks. It would hardly be worth the effort." Sage shook his head in wonderment.

"Maybe he didn't know how poor you are," said Tinna.

The crunch of rocks under tires announced the arrival of a car. Sage peeked out a window at the marked sheriff's car. The next two hours were spent telling his story and showing the deputies around. When enough deputies arrived, they made a sweep around the building, but no sign of the assailant was found. An exhaustive search of the studio finally revealed a bullet hole near the ceiling in the wall behind where Sage was standing. The guy had cranked off a shot in his direction. Using Sage's mobile painting stand, a deputy retrieved the slug. Preliminary indications were that it was from a 9mm.

Another aspect of the burglary was that the van used was a rental. At that hour of the night, they couldn't find out much about it. Finally, the deputies departed. There was still a little bit of the night left. Sage didn't think it was a good idea for Tinna to return to her kiln and she immediately agreed.

"In the corner of the granary is a set of bunk beds. When I had a man and his son working on the ceiling on this place, they slept out there. I'll make up a bed and you can get a little sleep before it gets light. Later this morning, we can check out the kiln."

Tinna followed Sage to the granary. Under a large canvas were the bunks. From a cabinet Sage pulled linen, a blanket, and a pillow. "You'll have to use the bathroom in the house. I'll see you later this morning."

When Sage awoke the sun was shining brightly. It was still early, but long past dawn. He wanted to roll over and forget about the morning, but too many Indians were standing on the ridge line. He crawled out of bed, plugged in the hot pot and headed for the shower. He was just building a rich shampoo lather when the bathroom door banged open.

"Sorry, but I couldn't wait." Tinna stepped into a stall, pulled down her bikini panties and sizzled. While doing so, Tinna was inspecting Sage and he began to react.

He didn't want to play the prude and turn to the wall so he continued his shampoo, but all he could manage was, "Good morning."

As Tinna peeled off a gob of toilet paper, she said brightly, "Good morning, I'm glad to see everything is functioning properly." She discarded the paper, stood up and snapped her bikini over a blonde thatch. "I heard the coffee water boiling. May I have a cup?"

"Help yourself."

Tinna adjusted her sports bra as she headed for the kitchen, leaving Sage with the provocative image of a 6'4"....she was wearing her cowboy boots....shapely blonde with an obscured, but well defined, chest and a barely hidden crotch. The memory continued to give him a problem during his shave. Returning to reality, Sage realized that at the moment there were other concerns more pressing than exercising his libido. Besides, he wasn't ready to enter into entangling alliances with Tinna, no matter how attractive the prospect might be, until a host of other factors was sorted out. He didn't think it was wise to get involved before he knew the pottery enterprise on his property was acceptable. If not, getting rid of it might be difficult if he was sleeping with the potter. Finally, he was able to wrap a towel around his waist so he could go for a cup of coffee. One of the coffee mugs was missing and so was Tinna.

Sage was stirring chili into his coffee when simultaneously the telephone rang and a fully dressed Tinna reappeared. Sage nodded to Tinna and said "Hello:" into the phone. The call was from Sergeant Langley, the detective from the preceding night.

"Mr. Grayling, does the name, L. Gehrig, mean anything to you?"

"No, unless you're referring to the legendary baseball player, Lou Gehrig."

"I rather doubt that's the one. He's dead, and this one is the one who booked a flight from LA to Albuquerque and then rented the van that we now have impounded. In less than two hours after his arrival in town he's pulling an arrow out of his ass. Do you have any idea what might be behind that kind of activity?"

"Yes," said a thoughtful Sage. "I would guess it has something to do with the murder of my boss in LA the day before yesterday. I would imagine Detective Fuente of the Sheriff's Office would like to hear about this. Wait a minute and I can get you his number."

Sage laid the phone on the table and headed for his bedroom. He had Fuente's business card in his billfold.

Tinna was almost treading on his heels as he went for the card. "Schießekompf! You're involved in a murder and didn't say anything about it. What happened?"

Sage waved her to silence as he picked up the office phone and gave the deputy the phone number. Tinna settled into Sage's reading chair, but she had her head cocked trying to pick up that part of the conversation that was in Sage's ear. Sage smiled, shook his head at the hungry display of curiosity. He hit the speaker phone button as the deputy was saying, "....haven't found any sign of your intruder. He didn't show up at any of the legitimate medical facilities for any treatment. There were no carjackings reported. There was no grand theft auto in your area. We patrolled the district and didn't find any bodies so we are working under the assumption he got away. This day and age, it's a pretty good bet that he had a cell phone so he could call for help."

"Did you get a description of him? I'll be going back to LA to finish a painting. Maybe I'll run into him there. I'd like to be able to make a connection."

"Everything is rather vague. He has a dark complexion, maybe Hispanic, medium height, strong build with broad shoulders, dark hair. Age guesses range from thirty to fifty....a young fifty. All I can come up with is that he was casually dressed."

"That description matches a good percentage of the males in LA," said Sage.

"We should eventually come up with a name on the guy. There was a ditty-bag in the van that we are assuming came from him. It had the latest copy of Sports Illustrated, a pair of medium sized white briefs and a whole bunch of pills. There should be some useable fingerprints in there as well as the van. Oh, yes, forensics didn't find any fingerprints at your place. He was probably wearing gloves when he was in the house."

"Interesting," said Sage. "But how did this joker get off a plane, rent a car, procure a ladder and a gun and find my house in two hours? Also, how did he know he would need a ladder to get into my house? On the surface, I'd say he was either clairvoyant or he had a local spotter. It also sounds as if he had the help of a local, because he got away from here and I'm pretty far out in the sticks. Plus, he didn't have any regular medical attention."

"I can't think of any way of finding an accomplice until we find out who he helped. When we come up with some identifiable prints then we may have a chance to connect up the local dots. I'll talk to Fuente and see if he has any ideas."

Sage signed off and turned to Tinna, "What's this scheißeknopf stuff? "

"Oh, I just transliterated a good old American term of endearment into German."

"Slick, slick, you sure weaseled out of that one.

Tinna smiled benignly. "Now tell me about the murder."

It was still a little early in the day to be running around in a wet towel, so as Sage began his narrative, he tossed the towel into the laundry corner and pulled on a pair of shorts and a

T-shirt. Tinna had already seen all there was to see. Anyway, Tinna hardly noticed. She was dividing her attention between the story and scrutinizing Sage's bedroom. That was the only room in the house he had decorated. Sage had taken one thirty-foot bedroom, plus the girls' bathroom and ten feet from the corner bedroom to create his pad. It was a huge area. Later, she found out it was twenty by fifty-five feet. At the south end, next to the door in to the bath was a wet bar with all the accouterments. Sage had put the plumbing from the girls' rest room to good use. It was bracketed by two walk-in closets, which would have been about the size of her apartment kitchen and bedroom. Along the west wall was a king sized bed. Further along that wall was a fireplace with a conversation circle of overstuffed chairs.

Tinna had parked on a recliner that was in the library section. The end of the closet and the east wall were lined with well stocked book shelves. On the other side of a door out to the portales was a U-shaped office assembly with all the modern equipment. The north wall was glass. Sliders divided the bedroom from the studio. The floors were old brick but with scads of sheep skins scattered about. She knew she was in a masculine lair. And, oh, the white sheepskins on the floor.

Sage had been watching the room survey, wondering if she was hearing anything he had said. That idea was put to rest when she started firing questions about various implications of things he had said, ending with, "Where do you stand now?"

"Probably, Fuente will be furious about me coming home. After they get to checking around, I can't see how they can keep me as a suspect. When they lift the restrictions on the house and let me have my car back, I'll go finish up the painting. Later, I'll call Bert to see what's been happening. It's got to be an outside job. I'm sure neither Bert nor Mrs. Bruckner killed Brand, and I know I didn't. When they find out about the break-in here, by a guy from LA that should help take me off their list."

"What about the sheriff? It sounds as if you're on his caca list."

"Oh, I can't see how he can give me a problem. I'm more worried about Anna Bruckner. What's he going to do if he finds out she's an alien?"

Sage headed for the door. "I'm starving to death. Let's get some breakfast. How do waffles sound? I'll have to get to the grocery store soon."

"That sounds good to me, but first I want to run out to check on the kiln. I know it will need more fuel by now."

"I'll go out there with you. That joker might still be skulking about."

Tinna straightened her back to achieve maximum height and stuck out her chest. "No, I can take care of myself. I'm a big girl."

"Yeah, I can see that," said Sage with a smile and a nod of his head.

Sage had regular coffee made, the orange juice thawed, and the batter ready when he heard Tinna head for the bathroom to wash off the cow chips. After breakfast, Tinna left to continue her work and Sage put in the call to Bert.

Bert greeted him with, "Boy, is your name mud around here. Fuente is furious. Not because you skipped out, but because your departure put him right in the line of the sheriff's wrath."

"I did just as I was told. What can he do to me? Are they making any progress on the case or just fuming at me?"

"Of course, they aren't telling me anything, but it looks like they are focusing a lot of attention on Tony Roskal and his associates. Oh, they've been checking on a lot of Dieter's business adversaries, but nothing apparently has come up. I'm fielding a lot of complaints from those businessmen about the police interrogations. All I can tell them is that the authorities have no idea who they are looking for, so they're checking anyone who had any connection to Dieter. They're still not happy."

"Any word when the house will be open?"

"Not yet. The press is getting on the sheriff's tail for lack of progress and it has only been a couple of days. As soon as the police tape comes down I'm going to have to lock the place up or we'll be swarming with reporters and cameramen. Part of it is just to be able to take pictures in this house to show how the rich live. I'm getting as many calls from home page reporters as crime reporters."

"Let me know as soon as you get some word that I can get back in."

"Okay. I hope it's soon. I could use your help with Anna. I don't speak German and she still wants to speak in her native language. She is really upset. Swain turned her in to the INS when he found out she was an alien. Immigration was here and Anna is not quite under house arrest. She can go to the grocery store but she's not supposed to leave the immediate area. She is very distraught. She likes you, and your presence would probably help. She needs someone to mother right now."

"Oh boy. Well, anything I can do. I like Anna."

While he was waiting around, Sage made contact with Luke Halliday, the manager of the Brand works in Dallas. He made arrangements to get into the house to see the wall, make his measurements and to photograph the land that would be represented. Luke said he would find all the old pictures of the view they used to have. Sage hadn't planned on going to Dallas until after the LA painting was complete, but when Bert reported that it still would be several days before he could return to the house, Sage booked a flight to Texas.

Luke's son, Sammy, picked up Sage from the airport. Sammy was home from college for the summer and dad put him to work. Sage had never been in Dallas before. And Sammy, who had seldom been out of the city, gave a running commentary on the geography and history of the area from the freeway that was whisking by them as they moved out of town into the countryside. Atop a hill rising out of the plain was the twin for Brand's house in LA.

There were some differences. Even though the driveways and paths were laid out on the same design, the landscaping conformed to locally indigenous plants. The surfaces of the houses gave variant appearances because of the climate. The LA site was much more humid. The aridity of Texas was reflected in the weathering of the paint.

Luke met the car at the front entry. Luke was tall and lanky.... much like Sage. Beyond that they were entirely different men. Luke was pure Texan from his drawl to the belt buckle holding up his jeans. Luke's office was in the same location as Bert's. The one difference was a small refrigerator loaded with Lone Star beer. Luke tossed a can to Sammy and told him to skedaddle. He handed Sage a beer before popping his own can.

"What's the latest word from LA? They figured out who done it yet?"

"My only source of information is Bert and you've probably talked with him since I have. The only tidbit I can add is that I had an intruder in my house that came directly from LA. I would suspect there is a connection." Sage went through the story of burglary.

Luke got a real kick out of Sage's actions. "Ha, you'd make a fine Indian. You put an arrow in his ass and almost deballed 'im with a fence post. Now, I call that good work."

Sage declined another beer and asked to see the wall he was going to paint. As they moved through the house Sage felt he was having a déjà vu experience. Everything was the same as in LA. The office had the same furniture arranged in the same manner. Brand's office door stood open revealing an identical desk and chair. The conference table hadn't been moved to accommodate the artist, but the new wall was the same as the one he was working on in California. Sage made some measurement to make sure the dimensions were the same. Luke took him out onto the balcony off the kids' rooms. The view was different..... yet the same. There was a flat plain below the hill instead of undulating hills, but it was covered with subdivisions leaving the view of a sea of rooftops. The house was situated in a slightly different position in relationship to the sun so the shadows were different. Sage took digital pictures of the room and of the scene that used to be overlooked from the room. While he was taking the photos he remembered he had taken shots of Brand and the murder scene. He had completely forgotten them in the rush of other events.

When Sage had finished his work, he returned to Luke's office. "That crystal chandelier is going to have to go. It is the same in LA. It casts sparkles of light on the painting that would deny the illusion I'm trying to create."

"I'll call the guy who did the wall and have him get a fixture that won't cause the problem."

"Did the same guy do the work in both houses?"

"Yeah, he's an old-world carpenter that Brand had known for a long time. He did the work here and then duplicated it in the LA house. Brand always wanted everything identical. Everyone was pleased with the arrangement. The boss closed down each house in turn and gave the staff a three-week paid vacation so they couldn't bug the contractor, who is a crotchety old bastard."

"Well, I've got to catch a plane. When I've finished in LA and have the cartoon ready for this place, I'll give you a call to make arrangements."

"Fine, there shouldn't be any problems. Sammy will drive you back to the airport."

Sage thought for a moment before asking, "Is Elke staying here?"

"Sometimes, why?"

"We had a run-in at the other house. She smeared a big peace sign in the middle of my wall, which raised the price a thousand bucks. I didn't lose money by repairing it, but I hate to do the same thing twice."

"I heard about that. She comes and goes. I can't very well keep her out of the house. But I can take any repair costs out of her allowance like Bert did. That might make her think twice before pulling another stupid stunt."

Luke doesn't think any more of her than Bert.

*****

Sage slept most of the way back to Albuquerque. He didn't like those turnaround flights, but there was no reason to stay any longer in Dallas. He could do his sketching much better in his own studio. He still was driving the rental car. In the morning, he'd return it and catch a ride with Tinna back to the house. He'd use his old van until he could get back to LA.

It was 10:00 pm by the time he got back to the studio. He drove around the building to make sure no vans or ladders were along the wall. He ran a check on the inside too. *I must be getting paranoid.* Everything was clear. After mixing a martini, he went to the bedroom office to check for any calls, emails or faxes. There was a call on the machine from Bert.

"Sage. You'd better get back here. They lifted the restrictions on the house. Fuente called to say that the sheriff has released your Caddy, but he's stipulated you have to pick it up before noon tomorrow or the impound supervisor is to call the salvage yard and have it taken away as junk. Fuente suggested you bring a flatbed tow truck. He wouldn't elaborate any further. Give me a call so I can pick you up when you arrive. Oh, yes, I'd suggest you have your ownership papers on the car. If you can't prove it's yours, they may not release it to you on your word. Give me a call."

It was five minutes before Sage could control his rage sufficiently to call the airlines for tickets. He was spending a fortune on those next-flight-out tickets. He dug out his birth certificate, passport with photograph and the title to the Caddy. He had time to take a shower and pack a carry-on bag. He turned in the rental car and had enough time before boarding to call Tinna, asking her to keep an eye on the house.

Bert's smiling face did a lot to dispel the black thoughts Sage had carried with him during the flight, which prevented sleep. He had been plotting.

"Welcome back to Los Angeles and all our smog," said Bert. "Traffic is pretty heavy, so we'd better move along. Do you have luggage?"

"No, I'm traveling light. Have you heard anything more about my car?"

"Not a word. I've made arrangements for a tow company to meet us there. I'm trying not to speculate on what Swain may have done. You can bet he's not done anything that can cause him any legal problems. He's good at covering his butt."

There was a flat-bed tow truck waiting at the impound entrance. It was a huge fenced yard stuffed with vehicles. On one side was a building complex with garage doors. Sage presented his ID and the ownership papers for the Cadillac to the man behind the desk, who seemed to find something funny when he found out which vehicle was involved. He didn't go beyond smirking. He processed the papers. As he handed the release to Sage, he said, "You have to have that stuff out of here in 48 minutes."

Sage stood in front of the counter minutely inspecting the clerk as if he were a bug specimen, taking in every little detail. The clerk lost his smirk and began fidgeting. Finally, he said, "You're wasting time. The sheriff said it had to be out of here by noon."

Sage wheeled around and headed out of the office with Bert on his heels. Sage gave the papers to a yardman, who also smirked. He pointed to the end of one of the buildings. "It's all there.... every nut and bolt.

Sage's classic Cadillac was sitting flat on the ground. It had been stripped down as far as possible without breaking any welds. All the pieces were stuffed into the vehicle or stacked on the rack above. The doors were off, as was the hood and trunk lid. The tires had been taken off the wheels and stacked where the seat had been. The seat was on the rack. All the painting materials had been moved around. Cans of paint had been opened and dumped into a big bucket. The bucket also proved to be holding all the nuts, bolts, screws and clips that had been removed.

Sage stood beside the car for a moment. Turning to Bert, who hadn't uttered a word, he said, "Get the tow truck in here." Sage turned back to the car and began taking a complete set of photographs of the mess. When he tried to take a picture of the yardman, he ducked and ran.

When the tow truck pulled in, the driver said, "Boy, I've seen some bad ones, but this beats them all."

"They do this frequently?" said Sage.

"Once in while. They say they're looking for drugs, but I think they're just pissed at the driver for some reason."

"We only have a few minutes to get this out of here. Get to work."

The truck operator lifted the front of the car and put dollies under until he could drag it onto the inclined bed. He had to stow loose items, but he was ready to roll with five minutes to spare.

Bert handed the driver a slip of paper. "Take the car to this address and give it to André."

As Sage followed Bert back to his car, Bert explained. "André is an old shade-tree mechanic who has worked on the family cars for years. Dieter lets him have space in one of the company buildings for a very nominal rent. André wouldn't think of not paying. I'd suggest leaving André to work his magic. He'll call when it's ready. You'll be charged for the work, but it'll be nothing compared to what the garages would charge. We have to get to the house. Anna is preparing lunch for us. She desperately needs something to do."

"What's her legal status?

"INS still has her under virtual house arrest. I think the only reason she's still here is that the sheriff thinks he may need her as a witness if they can come up with the murderer."

"Are they any closer to finding him?"

"I don't think so. Of course, they don't tell me much, but from their actions they are still flopping around trying to find someone to hang it on. Their focus continues to be on Tony Roskal. As far as I can tell, they don't have anything to really cause them to look in his direction. I think they are using the murder as an excuse to poke into his affairs. This has a bit of a risk. Both Swain and Webster are Democrats. They'll be competing for the same job. The unions are staunch Democratic supporters.

"If they push Roskal too hard and he's not their boy, then one or both may lose union support, which could put a crimp in campaign financing."

Sage gave Bert a more detailed report of the burglary in Albuquerque than he had given over the phone.

"Have the authorities found L. Gehrig?"

"I hear that was a false name. But so far as I know, they haven't found anyone with an arrow hole in his butt."

Bert parked by the kitchen. Anna greeted Sage as if he were a long lost son. The German flowed like flood waters. Sage wanted to go upstairs to check on his painting, but she would not hear of it. The food was getting cold. It had to be eaten immediately.

Lunch could well have been a full dinner for eight. Finally, Sage was able to stagger away from the table to head upstairs. Bert gave him a parting shot. "Things are pretty messy up there."

Since there were no longer windows in the room, it was dark. Sage snapped on the overhead lights as he entered and then stopped in his tracks. Now he knew why Bert and Anna had insisted he eat before going upstairs. There was black fingerprint power smeared all over the world. There were black smudges and smears over a good percentage of his painting. His whole paint caddy and working surface was befouled with fingerprint powder. All of his tools, ladders, and lighting equipment were dirty. It was wanton vandalism. Sage had no doubt where the order had originated. Fingerprint powder was one of the hardest things in the world to clean up. First his car, and now this.

Sage returned to the kitchen where both Bert and Anna were rigidly awaiting his reaction.

Sage pulled the digital camera out of the bag he'd left in the corner and without a word returned to the office and began recording the damage.

For two days he cleaned. Since he didn't have his car, he spent all the days and most of the nights removing the powder from his world. He didn't have much to say to anyone. After he'd removed all the loose powder from his painting, he turned to his equipment. It was cleansed thoroughly. The top had been left off his palette, exposing the paint to the air so he had to scrape off the hardened paints and lay out fresh colors. His brushes had been removed from the turpentine. They had hardened. Since his extra brushes were in Dreadnought, Sage called in an order to an art store. Bert picked them up for him.

Finally, Sage was ready to repaint the damaged area. He positioned his lights to cover the far right of the painting. As he stood back to reestablish his perspective, he noticed a stain on the white tile floor in the right corner of the room under his painting. Closer inspection suggested it was a dried puddle. Sage pulled a couple of paper towels from a roll and sloshed some bottled water on the pad. He wiped up the stain. The smell indicated it was urine. Thinking back he couldn't remember ever seeing any little dogs or cats in the house. Closer inspection didn't reveal any stains on the walls or his painting.

Sage started to throw the towels into the garbage can he'd appropriated for the cleaning job, but things didn't quite add up, so he went to the kitchen where Anna gave him a quart-sized zip top plastic bag. He sealed the towels in the bag and tucked it away in his paint caddy.

Later, when Bert stopped by, Sage asked, "Do you have any little dogs or cats in the house?"

"The kids had all sorts of pets. Especially Elke, who loves animals, but there haven't been any around here for years."

"No, this would have had to have been while the police had possession of the house. Something peed in the corner. I'd accuse the sheriff, but there wasn't a big enough volume and he didn't hit the painting. Maybe it wasn't urine at all." Sage let the subject drop.

That evening, Sage again took a look at the corner. He became convinced that the liquid had not been deposited in the room, but it had come under the wall. He went into the adjoining room.... Karl's bedroom. The room was carpeted and there was no sign of any liquid being spilled against the common wall.

Sage went onto the balcony and looked around the edge to

where the windows into the office had been bricked up. There was nothing there to account for the leakage. Besides, there hadn't been any rain and the wall was high above the irrigation system. Returning to the office, he pulled a chair from the table to sit contemplating the situation. There was something wrong, but he couldn't get a handle on it. He went back into Karl's room and then returned to the office to take another look at the intervening wall.

In his tool kit, he had a thirty-foot tape measure. He measured Karl's room and the width of the balcony. He added the distance from the wall of Karl's room to the entry to the office. Then he measured from the entry to the office to the wall he was painting. There was nearly four feet missing. The thickness of the outer wall would eat up eight inches or so, depending on the construction. Sage's conclusion was that there was an open area behind the wall he was painting.

A minute inspection of the wall showed that the left hand half of the new wall had no caulk around the edges. The seams were very tight, but not filled. The right half had been caulked. That might have been a contractor's mistake, but for some reason he doubted it.

If the left side of the wall was the hinge side of a door, there could be no caulking. A door might also explain those molding strips he had to "live with."

He owned an electronic stud-finder, which he used to locate structural members when he had to hang large paintings. But it was in his car. The thought of his dismembered Dreadnought brought back black thoughts.

Because of all the things that had happened since the murder, Sage had fallen far behind. He put considerations of the wall construction out of his mind and returned to repairing the painting. He buried himself in his work. He ate when Mrs. Bruckner put food in front of him and napped when necessary. On the fifth day after his return to LA, André called to say the Caddy was ready. He delivered it while Bert and Sage were eating lunch. Everyone trooped out to see what miracles André had wrought. Sage was truly delighted. Dreadnought sat in all its gleaming glory. Everything was back in place and André had given it a high wax job. The rack on top had a new paint job covering all the accumulated mars and scratches plus the new ones added when the impound mechanic had thrown all the body parts on top.

Sage was truly impressed by the transformation from the disembodied hulk he'd found at the impound compound to the gleaming car of his dreams. To keep from getting emotional he busied himself with the meticulously kept two-and-a-half-page record of the work performed. André had not only put everything back together, but fixed items that needed attention, such as a leaky brake cylinder, cracked fan belt and a host of other deficiencies. The $2753.12 figure at the end was going to hurt his budget, but Sage considered himself fortunate that it wasn't several times higher.

André said he didn't take credit cards, so Sage climbed into Dreadnought and fumbled with the shelf he had built from the back of the front seat to the rear window after he'd removed the rear seat and wall to the trunk. The construction enclosed the storage area below and provided a carrying platform for paintings and other flat cargo. There was a snapping sound and Sage raised a portion of the platform revealing a thin voided area, which contained an assortment of items, including Sage's check book.

The hilarity of the moment struck Bert, who erupted into laughter. "You mean they tore your car apart and they never found you cache? What boobs!"

Sage was glad to see even Mrs. Bruckner smile over the image. The strain of the last few days had really taken a toll on her. She was definitely looking her age now, where before, age never seemed to relate to her.

André accepted his check and Bert offered him a ride back to the shop. With his wheels back, Sage felt as if a weight had been removed from his shoulders. He told Mrs. Bruckner he'd be going out for dinner and a movie that evening.

In recent days, Sage had had his fill of heavy, German style food, so he chose a seafood place. He dined on shrimp. He'd already checked the movie schedule so he had a destination in mind as he went to the parking lot.

He found a young, slender built man leaning against the front fender of his car. As he approached, the man straightened up and said, "Mr. Grayling?"

Sage acknowledged his name.

"Mr. Roskal would like to have a word with you." The man bobbed his head toward the rear of the lot where a large, dark sedan sat, looking sinister in the fading light. Sage hesitated.

"This is a request. I extend requests. If it had been a command appearance, Tiny would have issued the order." The man bobbed his head toward the rear corner of the restaurant where a hulking form was leaning against the wall. "Mr. Roskal would like to talk to you about a common problem."

Although Sage was more than a little apprehensive, he moved toward the sedan while surveying available assets and escape routes. The young man opened the rear door. Sage had to bend down to see inside. Seated on the far side of the car was an immaculately dressed man. He appeared to be in his fifties. Physically, he was much shorter than Sage and tending to the portly side, although he still looked as if he would be a real problem in a street fight.

"Mr. Grayling, do sit down. I would like to investigate the possibility we could be mutually helpful to one another. I'm Anthony Roskal, and you and I have a similar problem.....Sheriff Harvey L. Swain."

Sage wasn't about to fold his elongated frame into a cramped iron box that could be full of hazards. "I'm too tall to fit comfortably into these economy cars. Roll down your window and we can chat." Without waiting for a reply he walked around the car.

When the window whined its way down, Sage leaned an elbow on the top, bent at the waist and said, "Good evening, Mr. Roskal. How can a union leader not love a good Democrat like Harvey L.

Swain?"

"Who says he's a good Democrat?" growled Roskal. "A good Democrat wouldn't try to bite the hand that feeds him."

"One has to be careful of offering a hungry, mad dog a tidbit. He's apt to lose a finger or two. But you didn't look me up to exchange philosophies. For his political future, Swain has to pin this case on someone and his choices are few. I'm one because I was there. You're another because you were locked in a battle with Brand over union jobs. What Swain doesn't realize is that you already lost the battle, so there was no reason to kill your opponent."

Roskal bristled. "What do you mean lost the battle? We haven't lost the battle."

"As soon as the technology became a reality, you lost the battle. You may be able to delay it for a bit, but that port will be built. You'd be better off trying to figure out how that new technology can benefit you and position yourself to take advantage of it. And don't send any more night visitors my way."

Roskal laughed hard enough to start his soft middle quaking. "You may have ruined a good boy. You almost shot Vic's balls off with that arrow and then when you chucked that tree through the window, he had more visions of singing soprano. He's still shaking over that. How'd you figure it out?"

"Who else could send a burglar out from LA into the sticks and have someone there to provide him with a gun and a ladder? Figuring out who wasn't hard, but why?"

"Like you say, Swain doesn't have many choices. I know I didn't have anything to do with Brand's death. I don't know about you. But, if the police were to find a $50,000 stash in your house, with the source of it pointing in another direction, then they'd quit giving me so much trouble."

"Oh, now that's really nasty."

"Nothing against you personally....business is business."

"After trying that little stunt, you're still looking to me for help?"

"Why not? Business is business. Both of us are still on the hook. I hear Swain has been making life miserable for you with your car and your painting. He's got a whole task force nosing into my affairs. It would be to our mutual advantage to get him to look somewhere else. I had to shake a tail to get here this evening and then change cars. I'm getting tired of all this attention."

"Well, for whatever good it's worth, I didn't have anything to do with Brand's death. I'm certain, in my own mind, that neither Mills nor Mrs. Bruckner had any hand in it. The sheriff has ruled out Brand's kids. They were off on frolics of their own. That leaves you and if it wasn't you, then the chances are good that it would be someone like you....a business adversary."

"I'm thinking pretty much the same way. That's why I set up this meeting. I want to know if you saw something or know something that I don't. You, being an outsider, may not recognize the value in something, where I might."

"You mean you're trying to solve Brand's murder?"

Roskal smiled. "I have ways of getting information that aren't open to the sheriff. It's not that I want to do his job, but I want to get him off my back. He's on a fishing trip under the guise of probing Brand's murder. If I can toss a murderer his way, I'll do so to get him to leave me alone."

"I'm not so sure he really cares about solving this case. He's a politician locked in battle with another politician, the DA. I wouldn't put it past Swain to devise some half-baked case against someone....you, me, someone...and turn it over to the DA for prosecution. Swain's done his job by finding the murderer. If Webster can't get a conviction, he gets the black eye. Swain gets the political hay no matter which way it goes."

"Yeah, that scenario had occurred to me too. Do you know anything that would help?"

"Like what?"

"You had chances to talk with Brand. Did he say anything that would indicate he had enemies? Did anyone come to see him? Did you see anything around the house that didn't look right?

Anything?"

"You're asking the same questions the detectives did. I didn't know anything that seemed to be of the slightest interest to them. Brand never discussed any business with me other than my painting. No one came to see him while I was there. I never overheard any phone calls. He talked on the phone in his office, but I couldn't hear anything and there never were any angry arguments. I'll even add this. I was with Bert Mills more than with Brand and there was never any indication of a problem. Neither of them were looking over their shoulders as far as I could see."

Roskal shook his head. "I'd hoped some name would pop up that might mean something to me."

"Oh, one name did surface several times."

"Who?"

"Tony Roskal. He was locked in a battle with Brand over the new port facility."

"Humph," said the union boss, as the tinted window went up. The young driver eased into the front seat and Tiny headed for another car parked among customer cars. The black car slid away into the darkness that had fallen.

It was too late to catch the movie he had planned on seeing and he didn't want to wait for the next go-around, so he headed home. Before going into the house, Sage hunted up his stud finder, a thin, three-foot welding rod, and a small drill bit. Mrs. Bruckner was in her room as Sage let himself in through the alarm system.

In the office, Sage tested the wall. It was a stud wall built on sixteen-inch centers. From the jumble of readings he was getting, the left half of the wall seemed to have additional structural members. He selected an area with a medium shade of green that reoccurs repeatedly in the painting. He drilled a tiny hole. He was able to push the entire welding rod, less the tip that he held in his fingers, into the hole. He moved to another location and repeated the process. This time he ran into something two feet in. He encountered several different depths in the eight holes he drilled.

Carefully, Sage filled the holes with dabs of spackle. In the morning, he'd obscure them completely with paint. Sage knew there was a room back there, but he couldn't find any way of getting into it other than bashing though the drywall with a hammer or cutting a hole with a drywall saw. Now he knew why he had to live with the molding strips. They covered the door seam. He toyed with the idea of asking Bert about it, but caution and his secretive nature prevailed.

The next morning, Sage went down for breakfast. Mrs. Bruckner had obviously been crying, but she refused to discuss any problem with him, even in German. Sage had grown very fond of the cook. He was trying to decide if he should press the issue, when the back door bell rang. It was Detective Fuente. Mrs. Bruckner let him in and immediately disappeared into her quarters.

Fuente was not in the best of humor. He started out the conversation with, "Smart-ass, you left town. I'm still on the sheriff's shit-list for not preventing you from leaving. Both of us have been paying the price ever since. The sheriff wants to see you downtown."

"Get a cup of coffee and let me finish my breakfast. I'll have to change out of my paint clothes before going out."

"This isn't a dress-up affair. He'd rather you look like a bum than be dressed up. But, I could use a cup of coffee. Finish your meal."

Fuente poured his coffee and sat down at the table. Sage slowed his eating and casually asked, "How's the case coming?"

"Lousy."

"What's he want to see me about?"

"The sheriff will tell you. One thing for sure is that he'll want to know all about the break-in at your house. The sheriff didn't know you'd left LA until that request for information came through from the deputy in Albuquerque. That set him off, and

I was first in line to get the full blast."

"Sorry you got in the way, but I wasn't going to waste my time just to please that arrogant son-of-a-bitch. I can see he's a politician. How is he as a sheriff?"

"He's a good politician," said Fuente, with a bleak smile. "And the politician in him is getting very nervous. The papers gave him a holiday until after the memorial service. Mills said that Brand's son didn't think it important enough to come to LA. The body was cremated and then there was a memorial service at one of the hotels. The sheriff still wouldn't let Bert use the house. But after the service, the media got back on his case. He's been making oblique statements and he's generally mysterious. Now everyone wants results. He has to show some activity on the case. At the moment you are that activity."

"So, this little interview is just a theatrical maneuver to sooth the reporters?"

"Gee, I wouldn't know anything about that," said Fuente in a mock theatrical manner. "Come on. It's time to move."

"I'd rather drive."

"I don't think that would be wise. You don't want the sheriff to get any further notions about the 'queer looking car'. I'll see that you get back."

Sage didn't know what to expect. He'd never been hauled in for questioning before. However, he certainly didn't anticipate he'd be ushered through the front door into the public waiting room, behind the counter, and directly to the sheriff's private office. Fuente knocked and when he got a response, he stuck his head in the door to say, "Grayling's here, Sir."

"Put him in five."

Fuente led the way into a back hall and opened the door that had a big number five painted on the wall. "Wait here."

Sage entered and Fuente closed the door. It was a small interrogation room with a table bolted to the floor and three chairs. There was a mirror on the wall, which Sage suspected was a one-way glass. There was a control panel built into the wall. Sage decided that the room was not a nice place. He pulled one of the chairs into the corner where he couldn't be seen through the window and prepared himself for a long wait. It only took a short time before a deputy stuck his head in the door to check to see if Sage was still there.

Forty-five minutes later, Swain came stomping into the room with a thunderous expression on his face. He was accompanied by Fuente. Swain sat in one of the chairs, but the detective leaned against the wall signaling his secondary status in the event. "Turn that chair around and sit up at the table."

"I need to go to the restroom," said Sage.

"You'll have to wait."

Sage sat down across the small table from the sheriff. "I bet I can fill up your shoe from here." Sage sat up straight, moved forward on his chair and spread his legs. He reached down to unzip his pants.

The sheriff slid back from the table. "Fuente, take this......take him to the latrine."

Sage followed Fuente to a men's room where Sage dribbled a few drops into a urinal much to the suppressed mirth of the detective. "Hombre, you know how to live on the edge."

An impatient sheriff was standing outside number five awaiting their return. Sage seated himself across from Swain who began ranting, "I ought to throw you under the jail where no one will ever find you. You knew you weren't to leave town and you go flouncing off to another state." As Swain continued along a similar vein, Sage reflected on the tragic state of affairs where our leaders were selected from this sort of a gene pool. When the sheriff finally wound down, Sage figured he'd be able to go as soon as he was contrite and he said, "Sorry, Sir." *You sad son-of-a-bitch.*

However, Swain wasn't finished. "I was about ready to drop you from the list of possible suspects, but now I find that would have been an ill advised move. I find that you are having clandestine meetings with a....shall we say....a person of interest in this case.

I want to know your connection with Anthony Roskal."

That son-of-bitch either has a tail on me or a bug on my car.

"What makes you think I have any connection with Roskal?"

"You people always think you are so smart. We have dates, times and photographs of your meeting."

Sage broke in. "What people are you talking about?"

Swain ignored the question and continued to throw questions for the next twenty minutes, which Sage in turn ignored. Fuente shifted position catching the sheriff's attention and shook his left wrist in a signal that Sage inferred had to do with time. The sheriff immediately stood up, put his fists on the table and leaned into Sage's face. "Be a smart-ass, but I'll get to the bottom of this yet." He stomped out of the room with the same grace he had entered. Fuente followed him and closed Sage in the room.

Ten minutes later, Fuente returned. "The sheriff says to take you back to Brand's."

As they came out the front door of the Sheriff's Office, there was a crowd of people. Sheriff Swain was conducting a press conference. There were TV cameras, still photographers and press people gathered around.

Swain was saying...."We have been very busy reinterviewing various persons of particular interest in this case in an attempt to resolve a variety of conflicts in their stories." Fuente and Sage had to skirt around behind the podium. As they did so, Swain paused for a significant moment to watch them pass out toward the parked car.

From the crowd someone said, "That's the artist."

Swain regained attention of the press by booming out in his commanding voice. "It will take a little time to put the pieces together, but rest assured, progress is being made."

Bastard, this is a staged PR stunt.

Sage had wondered why Fuente had parked in visitors' parking instead of the sheriff's lot behind the building. Now he knew. He was being used as a pawn in the sheriff's little game. Instead of following Fuente to the car, Sage peeled off and sidled into the crowd before Fuente knew he was gone. Sage stood in the center of the group as the sheriff tried to conclude his remarks without showing his anger at seeing Sage towering above all the reporters.

As soon as the sheriff left the microphones, the reporters fell on Sage. Someone asked him to spell his name, which he did. "I'm a tromp l'oeil painter." He had to spell that and tell what it meant.

"Were you being reinterviewed, as the sheriff put it?" asked someone.

In a voice loud enough for all to hear, he said, "I really can't say anything. I doubt if the authorities would take kindly to me discussing their case. All I can say is that the sheriff didn't make a pass at me." In a lower voice, as if to himself, he said, "Of course, I was fully dressed this time and there were too many people around."

Sage started wading through the clamoring reporters, who now thought they had a juicy tidbit, toward Fuente who was standing with his palms turned upward and looking to the sky saying, "Why me?"

After they made good their retreat, Fuente lapsed into a Spanish tirade on death wishes, visitations from Diablo and finally he began imploring the Virgin of Guadalupe for deliverance from Sage's evil influence. He was still mumbling to himself when he dropped Sage at the front gate of the Brand property.

Bert was still at the house. Sage was as furious as Fuente, but his anger took him in a different direction....toward Swain. Bert had enough sense to refrain from comment until Sage got through venting. Sage related what had happened and gave his impression of how he'd been used. Sage's main immediate concern was the possibility of his car being bugged. Roskal had lost his tail and changed cars, so to find him and Roskal together, Sage must have been tailed either directly or by electronic means.

"What are you going to do?" asked Bert.

"Somehow I've got to find how they tailed me. I think Roskal had Tiny tailing me to the restaurant. He was in his own car. But, how did Swain's people get there? Were two cars following me? Or is there a bug? I don't even know what to look for."

"Let's save some time. I'm going to leave the house now and call André on my cell phone. He should still be at his shop. I'll lay out a route there and then watch to see if anyone is behind you. We'll let André check for a bug. He should know one when he sees one."

By the time Sage drove into the auto shop, it was rather obvious there was no car tailing them because the route was clear enough to have been able to spot anyone and there were no parallel fox and hounds routes.

André put the Caddy on a hoist and after a minute inspection of the underside, he declared it to be free of any bug that could have been attached in a walk-by. From the time it had been delivered, until Sage headed out for dinner, there hadn't been any opportunity to do anything other than slap a transmitter in a wheel housing or onto a bumper.

Sage had felt certain there must be a bug. André maintained that the car was clean of any small, battery operated variety, but pointed out the sheriff had had ample opportunity to install one while the car was at the impound garage.

"There's got to be a power source," muttered André as he started his inspection of other areas. A few minutes later the mechanic crawled out from under the dash with an "aha! The new Cadillacs have Navstar systems. Someone just wired one of those units behind the dash and hooked it up to the antenna. It's powered off the ignition so it broadcasts every time you are running the car. If I'd been working in that area and saw it, I'd have figured you'd just installed a unit to update the Caddy. It'll only take a moment to get it out."

"Oh, I don't want it out. Although, I do want to know how to disable the thing, when I want to."

"You want to leave it working?" said Bert.

"Sure, maybe I can have some fun with it. As long as I know it's there, I can't be hurt by it. If I want to do something where I don't want company, I'll turn it off.

Before he left the auto shop, André installed a hidden switch. Sage learned all about the unit and what it could do. While he remained in LA, he'd let the Sheriff's Office waste time charting his activities.

Two days later, Bert came up to look at the completed painting. Sage needed to put a finish coat over the top, but that would have to wait for a few days while the paint set up. After the inspection, Sage stowed his equipment in the corner of the room. He would return home to work on the drawing for the Texas house.

At dinner time, Sage tossed his bags into the car, drove past the seafood restaurant where he had met Roskal before. He turned off the bug and headed on out of town playing a long shot that the Sheriff's Office might think another meeting was taking place. Sage frequently began his trips in the evening because he'd rather drive at night without all the traffic to worry him.

Chapter 6

—ᜉᜉ—

The old, hulking adobe structure that he lovingly referred to as the Hacienda was a welcome sight as it came into view through the scrub brush. When it had been a caved-in shell, it had whispered to him. Now that it held out the rain and wind, it was humming a beautiful tune at the root of his consciousness. One day, he would make her sing again. He drove in a circuit around the structure to check if everything was all right, but really he just wanted to see her again. Along the back wall near the granary door was a huge pile of refractory bricks and other masonry materials. It was obviously Tinna's stuff, but the truck was not there. He detoured to the ana gama site. It had changed character considerably. It no longer looked like an abandoned archeological site. A makeshift plywood door had been added to the storage shed. A bright blue tarp covered a substantial pile of cow chips. There was no firing going on at the moment.

Sage parked Dreadnought in the garage. The kitchen table was loaded with mail. Tinna had been keeping track of things. A circuit of the main house revealed nothing out of order. There was, however, a change in the granary. Sitting in the middle of the parking area was a bright yellow, MGTD. In the corner of the vast room opposite the outer door was a fantasy forest of large ceramic pieces. They were nowhere close to what one would consider utilitarian pieces. They were indeed sculptural in nature. Many had been fired in separate pieces and put together to achieve their ultimate size and complexity. Glazes had been drizzled down them, giving a familiar effect, which he couldn't quite place.

Near the bunk beds in the other end of the building was a large stack of boxes and assorted household items, such as a vacuum cleaner and ironing board. Sage got a prickly feeling he had just been invaded. He had space, space, space and more space in the Hacienda, but he had no intention of sharing it with a roommate. He valued his privacy too much. His schedule around the house was to have no schedule. He did everything on his own time. He wasn't about to mesh schedules with anyone else.

As Sage stalked back to the house, he was thinking grizzly thoughts. He got out a bottle of gin but decided it was too early for a martini, so he grabbed a beer from the refrigerator. He pulled a trash can up to the table as he sorted through the mail. It was nice not to have to make a trip to the post office to retrieve the mail that had accumulated during his trips. That was one benefit to having Tinna around.

He retrieved his luggage from Dreadnought before heading for the office. There was a mountain of bills that clamored for payment. Some of them were already overdue and he'd have to pay late fees. It was going to be more difficult because of all the expenses he had had due to that bastard of a sheriff. But, none of those charges showed on his bill, yet.

A review of the telephone messages and faxes didn't produce any possibilities for future work. He still had the Texas job. If nothing unexpected happened, he could stay solvent for a few more months. Sage always had a stash of money set aside because on any commission there were inevitable outlays of cash necessary before ever getting the down payment. He had home improvement plans that would need a pot full of money, so he was interested in making more than just his job costs and living expenses.

One item of business that had to wait until he returned home was to run his digital camera cards, containing the photos of the crime scene and Dreadnought, through his computer and make prints. He selected the best of the shots and queued them to the printer. He stuck a stack of glossy paper in the tray and hit the print button.

He heard the rumble of Tinna's flat bed truck. There was no toot of the horn. It was still daylight and there was no outward sign he had returned. He immediately turned on the CD player and cranked up the sound so that Bartok's "Miraculous Mandarin" reverberated through the Hacienda. He wanted to avoid any embarrassing incidents.

It wasn't very long until there was a shout, "Is there a man in the house?"

Tinna was waiting in the passageway between the back yard and the house. She had not intruded into his space without invitation. Sage abandoned the printer and shouted back, "Is there a damsel in distress?"

Standing tall in her cowboy boots, with her shoulders thrown back, Tinna was about to bristle at the damsel reference, but controlled her response and broke into a smile as Sage came out of his lair. "Welcome back. Are you going to offer a lady a cup of coffee as she listens to all those wild tales of jousting with dragons?"

"That will take at least two cups of coffee." Sage led the way into the kitchen.

"You've probably already seen the tons of junk in the granary," said Tinna. "Before you tell me about all of your dragon slayings, I'd better explain. Just after you left I started a firing in the kiln in the garage of my apartment. This was a major firing for the fall show. The kiln got to woofing a bit and a neighbor reported me to the fire inspector. That bitch made me shut down the kiln and I ruined weeks of work. Then that govnjuk, *(shit head)* landlord and I got into a big fat fight and I got kicked out. It didn't take long to move my personal scheiße but tearing down the kiln and moving my pottery studio was the problem.

"On such short notice, I didn't have anywhere else to put it, so it's here. For the last few nights I've been sleeping in the bunk bed in the granary. Today, I hauled the last load of refractory material out. I still have to have the gas company move the big propane tank. I'll make other arrangements as soon as possible."

Sage circumvented commenting on the situation by asking, "How have the cave firings gone?"

"There are a couple of problems. I haven't been able to reach the temperatures I had hoped. The cow chips are too slow burning. I think I could get the temperatures up there with a blower, but I'm afraid that would take so much fuel, I'd be plowing around the desert all the time. The other problem is that access is too restricted and the firing chamber is too small for my big pieces. I love the concept, but execution is the problem. Everything is too small. I'd like to build a big ana gama out of brick, like this house is built. I'd make it a walk-in. If I built it myself, I wouldn't have to be afraid of cave-ins."

As Sage poured the coffee, Tinna changed the subject. "Have they caught the murderer yet? With my forced move, I haven't heard any news reports lately."

"No. As far as I can see, they haven't a clue about who did it. All the sheriff can do is harass people who I know didn't do it.... including me. Bring your coffee. I'll show you what they did to Dreadnought."

The printer was still cranking out large colored prints. It hadn't gotten to the Caddy pictures yet. Sage started to go through the murder scene photos, explaining to Tinna what she was seeing. When he got to the one showing his painting, Tinna expressed delight over what she could see of it behind all the painting paraphernalia. Sage rummaged through a drawer for a magnifying glass. In the right corner of the room there was a refraction of the flash off a shiny surface on the floor.

Sage pointed out the highlight to Tinna. "I know how the killer got in and out of the house."

"That shiny spot tells you that?" said an incredulous Tinna.

"When I got back from Albuquerque, I found a yellow ochre stain on the white tile floor. I thought a dog or cat had peed there, but there are no animals in the house. I wiped up the stain and it smelled like urine. I have the towels tucked away. I think the urine came under that wall. I poked around and there is a vacant space of three to four feet back there. It is my theory, the murderer knew about a secret room that was constructed when the windows were blanked out. I think the murderer entered after I left the house and before Mrs. Bruckner turned on the alarm and then left after she turned it off the next morning. Anyone knowing the house schedule could easily get in and out without anyone seeing him. That means the murderer was behind that wall for about twelve hours. I think he had to pee and did so in the corner."

"Who knows about this?"

"You and I."

"Oh caca, what are you going to do about it?"

"I have to go back to LA in a week or ten days to finish the painting. Before then, I'm going to Dallas to check my sketch for the other wall and I'm going to find out about that room. I don't want to have to cut a hole in my painting to get in there."

"You're already in trouble with the sheriff. What's he going to do when he finds out you know about that room? That's withholding information on a crime. Isn't that illegal here?"

"I'm going to make that SOB look like a horse's ass. Check those prints coming out right now. How would you like someone to do to your Daisy what he did to Dreadnought?"

Tinna ruffled through the car prints. "He did this to your car? Why?"

"Because I crossed him. He also took the opportunity to install a tracking device in Dreadnought."

"Pendejo! Boil his balls!" cried Tinna with feeling.

Sage gave a little, involuntary shudder. "As soon as I can set up an appointment with Luke Halliday, I'll be heading for Texas. This time I'll drive. The sun's going down. I'm going to have a martini. What can I fix for you?"

"I'll have a martini too, but with vodka."

As Sage mixed the drinks, he casually said, "When they made you shut down the kiln, what did that do to your fall inventory?" Sage knew that a good part of Tinna's annual income came from a major show in Phoenix.

"It was bad. I'll be short this year. I spent too much time on the ana gama. Then I had to press to get new work out and dried. Two firings would have put me in good shape, but I lost one whole load when I had to cut it off or go to jail. All those pieces are damaged. I have another load ready to go, but now I have no kiln. I had to dismantle it or lose it."

"How long will it take you to rebuild the kiln?"

"A lot longer than it took me to tear it down," said Tinna ruefully.

"Would it be of any help to rebuild your kiln out back in the brick yard?"

Tinna took a sip of the martini that Sage had just handed her. She was silent for a moment before answering. "It would be a great location, but I need electricity."

"There's a hundred feet of underground number ten Romex in the granary. You'd have to buy another couple of hundred feet. For the moment, it could be run on top of the ground and be buried later. That wouldn't give you a lot of juice, but it would run a blower and some lights."

"A kiln is a pretty permanent installation. You'd let me put it back there?"

"I told you, I have no plans for that area and that you can use it. That offer still stands."

Tinna was still trying to tell how serious Sage was. Previously, if anything went wrong, she wasn't losing anything but some labor in digging the ana gama kilns. She'd have a lot more invested if she set up her major firing operation back there.

"There's a lot more to it than just building the kiln. Even with a kiln, I'm out of business until I can find another location where I can set up my pottery. I have enough for another firing, but it is not worth building the kiln for that one shot. I've got to get back to creating new pieces. I need storage for them to dry. Then they have to be glazed. Once they're fired, I have to store them again. Besides, I need a place to live."

"If you could get back into production, could you still get enough inventories ready for the Phoenix show?"

"Oh yes, there's still time, providing I can find a place to set up shop. However, finding something I can afford is a problem. The fire marshal says I have to be either in an industrial zone or agricultural zone, and industrial rentals are expensive. They usually don't permit living on the premises without special permit. Many of my friends have gone through the same thing. If I can't stay where I'm working I have to rent a second place to live. That's too much money for me."

"If it would be of any help, you can convert that storage shed into a pottery. We can put a roof on it. That would give you a place to work and fire your pieces. Until you can make other arrangements, you can continue to sleep in the granary. You can work on your pieces in the granary until we can get a roof on the shed. There is no water or plumbing in the granary so you'd have to use the bath in here. You can use the kitchen if you provide your own food and clean up after yourself. Of course, as soon as the weather turns cold, the situation will change. There is no way that granary can be heated. It's too big. Working in the shed would be too cold too....unless some heat is brought in.

"I'm going to be gone quite a bit. When I finish the LA job, I'll then go on to Texas. I would appreciate someone looking after the place while I'm gone. When it was just a ruins, it didn't matter too much if someone broke in, but now I've accumulated too much stuff to let someone walk off with it."

Tinna gradually broke into a smile as she mulled the offer around in her head. She held up her glass and said, "I just may be able to get a reasonable show together for Phoenix....if no other disasters occur. Thank you."

Sage raised his glass back. "Good luck."

Both were silent for a bit, wondering if they were headed in the right direction. Sage broke the silence. "I've got to get something to eat before I attack that pile of stuff on my desk. Are you brave enough to take potluck on what I can find in the kitchen?"

"Sure, we Icelanders have cast iron stomachs."

From the freezer, Sage pulled a pack of stuffed clams and a bag of petite frozen peas. From a cupboard he produced a pack of Fettuccine Alfredo. "Put the clams on a plate and stick them into the big microwave. They take two minutes each. Sage put a pot with a measured amount of water for the noodles on a hot plate. The peas went into another microwave, set for six minutes, but he left the door open until the clams were half done.

Tinna was directed to the location of the placemats and flatware. Fifteen minutes later, the food was on the table and Sage was refreshing the coffee cups.

Chapter 7

Following dinner, Sage called Luke Halliday at home. After an exchange of pleasantries, Sage asked, "When would it be convenient for me to come down to make a final check on my layout?"

"I wouldn't do so until the beginning of the week. All hell has broken out here. The attorney just read the will to the kids. They are screaming mad. They're not going to get all Dad's money to blow. Not only that, it would appear that Karl and Elke had some private agreement between them that they would split up the property so Karl would get all the California real estate while Elke would take Texas. I don't know what that is all about, but when the property all went into the trust, it apparently disrupted some important plans.

"There is also a big legal battle brewing. The estate maintains that Texas was Brand's principle residence because the tax hit will be substantially smaller than in California. It appears California will challenge that contention. It will be tied up for years before any conclusion will be reached. That is one reason why your painting is important. The estate doesn't want it to appear that Dieter favored the California residence more than the Texas one by ordering an expensive piece of art work for his secondary home."

"What is supposed to happen by the weekend to clear the way for me?"

"By then Karl will have in his hand that chunk of money that was saved for him. He's off to Hydra, Greece, for a big party. He'll leave Sunday. Elke has taken up residence in the master bedroom, but she and her friend are supposed to attend some important march or rally, so she should pull out Monday morning."

"How about if I show up on Tuesday....say midmorning?"

"That would be fine. With all these legal battles being waged, I have a lot of office work to do. Come to the Brand house."

When Sage hung up, he had a firm date. Now he could lay out a schedule. He would have to spend some time finishing up the drawing, but he had three days at his disposal. He decided to see what he could do to help Tinna get back into production.

While Tinna was laying out the base for her kiln next to the shed, Sage strung wire to give her electricity. He also spliced a couple of concrete forms from the house roof construction project together and found enough leftover rebar to cast a ridge pole for the shed. The gas company delivered Tinna's oversized gas tank and set it behind the shed. Sage ran pvc pipe from his water tank to the back door of the granary, getting water much closer and more available. Later, when he had more time, he'd get a ditch witch and bury both the electrical wire and the pipe.

Just before Sage climbed into Dreadnought to head east, he helped Tinna mount the kiln door and the stovepipe. She still had to finish installing the burners.

*****

Luke tossed Sage a Lone Star beer as he walked into the office. Of course, that action shook up the beer just enough so one had to be careful how he opened the can. Sage had made that observation on his first visit while watching Sammy deftly open a tossed can. Luke made note that the lesson had stuck.

After some small talk and a rather lengthy discussion of

the murder, Sage got into the reason for the trip. "In addition to checking the drawing, I need to talk with your old world carpenter. I've run into some surface idiosyncrasies in painting on his wall. I've been worrying that there could be some material or technique that might not be compatible with my painting materials. I'd hate to have you call me up in six months to say the surface is effervescing or the paint is falling off the wall. I want to be on the safe side. Could you see if he's available and how I can get to him?" Sage didn't tell Luke the real reason for the visit, because whoever set up the murder had to know about that room in LA. The list of those who could have known is pretty short. He wanted to find out all he could about the rooms from the carpenter before he confided in any of the principals.

Luke swung back to his desk and consulted a PDA, for the number. The phone was answered by the carpenter's wife. Sage gathered that Heinz would be home a 4:00 pm and he'd be available then. Sage got the address and instructions on how to get to the Schueller house.

Sage left Luke in his office while he went upstairs to the large office. Just to make sure there was another secret room, Sage measured the distances. The measurements were the same for both houses. Sage made some final adjustments on his drawing before returning to Luke's office.

Since he hadn't eaten and the Schueller house was a considerable distance away, Sage took his leave after making an appointment to be back at the house at ten in the morning. The Brand house was a considerable distance out of town. Dieter had owned most of the land in that part of the county, but a sizeable tract had gotten away from him when an heir to the property found a builder to develop the property into upscale housing. That was the view that Dieter had wanted to block out by closing off the window in the office.

When Sage got into a commercial area, he selected a motel, checked in, and headed for the restaurant. He was able to catch a catnap before heading for the carpenter's house. With good directions, he had no trouble finding a beautifully maintained house in a modest residential area. Heinz Schueller met him at the door. He was a white-haired man of average stature. But he looked as if he could lift the corner of a house to repair the foundation. Sage could never remember ever shaking hands with a person whose flesh felt so dense. In contrast to the stony physical appearance, Heinz was warm and friendly despite his reputation of being craggy. When Mrs. Schueller asked her husband in German if she should offer a beer, he said no. But when Sage said he'd love a beer, indicating he understood them, he became a long-lost friend.

They retired to an airy back porch on the shade side of the house. Sage got right to the point. "Mr. Schueller, Luke told you I was the one doing the painting on your walls. I'm not having any problem with the surface. What I need to know is how to get into that secret room behind the wall."

That statement caught Schueller off guard. He reacted before he could cover his expression. He tried to regroup. Sage didn't give him time to lie. "I know there is a void behind the wall. I have probed it with a rod. I don't want to cut a hole in my painting, so I came to Dallas to cut my way through the wall here. I want you to tell me all about the rooms. Mr. Brand isn't around to care about the secret rooms."

Schueller thought for a moment before launching into his story. "I have done work over the years for Mr. Brand. He was a good man. He asked me to blank out the windows and then build a secret room along that wall. He cleared out both houses while I worked so no one would know about them."

"What were the rooms for?"

"Mr. Brand had many valuable things, but they were disappearing. He wanted a place to put them so they would not disappear. He also wanted a place to hide his fine wines so his son would not throw a party with his wines."

"How do you get into the rooms?"

"Why should I tell you? You are not part of the family. This should be family business."

"I'd like you to tell me for several reasons. There are only two members of the family left and I suspect both of them were the reasons why Mr. Brand had the rooms built. Another one is that I am being investigated for murdering Mr. Brand, which I did not do. The most important reason for me to get into those rooms is that the murderer hid in the LA room before and after the murder. I want to find out who. Whoever killed Mr. Brand had to know about that room. Who besides you and Mr. Brand had that knowledge?"

"No one."

"You didn't tell anyone?"

"Absolutely not."

"Do you think Brand told anyone?

" I don't think so, but I have no way of knowing."

"Would he have told Karl or Elke?"

"Absolutely not."

"How about Luke and Bert?"

"Mr. Brand said he wasn't going to tell anyone."

"Can you think of anyone else he would have told?"

"No."

"Then follow this line of thinking. If only you and Brand knew of their existence and Mr. Brand is dead, then who waited in that room to kill Brand?"

Schueller's eyes got big.

"This isn't my thinking, but I know it will be the sheriff's thinking. I had hoped to figure out who killed our boss to get the sheriff off our backs. To keep both of us out of trouble, I'd suggest you give me all the information you have."

It wasn't much of a leap to a state of cooperation. "Mr. Brand had me design those rooms for his own private use. No one else was supposed to know about them."

"How do you get into them?"

"There is a brass wall lighting fixture on each side of the fireplace. The switch is in the one on the right. There are four decorative nuts holding it on the wall. Unscrew the lower left one about three-eights of an inch and push. The left half of the wall swings in. The hinge is on the left wall. There are shelves along the inside wall. I don't know what Mr. Brand put in there. When I left, the rooms were empty."

"How do you close them?"

"Pull the nut back out and screw it down tight. There is a thin piece of metal under the edge of the door. When it opens the metal is exposed. Pull that to close the door. After you shut the door, tuck the strip back under the door."

"Can it be opened and closed from the inside?"

"Sure. There is a release so it can be activated from the inside. The door has to be closed to get to the shelves on the left side. They are behind the open door."

"Are there lights in there?"

"Yes, ceiling lights in both halves."

"When the door is opened is there any noise?"

"There is only the slightest of snaps as the electrical latch releases. The doors open and close by hand. There is no motor to make noise."

"Besides me, has anyone shown any interest in the walls or asked you about the rooms?"

"No."

"Not even Luke or Bert?"

"No."

"Mrs. Bruckner?"

"I do not know her. She was on vacation while I was there."

"For the time being, I'm not going to tell Luke about the room. I would suggest you not mention it either. It would complicate my inquiries because at the moment, he is not supposed to know. If he shows any signs of having that information, then we can suppose it came from some other source....maybe before the murder."

The next day, Sage met Luke at the house. Sage explained that the reason the wall felt different was that instead of sanding down the drywall compound, Heinz trowels it down and makes a smooth and compacted surface instead of a roughed up one. The two men chatted a while about the murder over a Lone Star beer before Sage took his leave saying he'd let Luke know when he was ready to start painting.

*****

Sage pointed Dreadnought's hood ornament toward the west. He drove through the night. When he pulled into the yard the next afternoon, Tinna's truck was not in sight. He parked Dreadnought in the garage. As he was passing though the jardin, he could faintly smell the distinctive odor of the start of a firing. He changed out of his travel clothes into grubbies and headed to the brickyard. The granary was much more orderly. Tinna had made a little living area around the bunk beds. A chair, small table, and a lamp were beside the bed. A rod bridged a gap in stacks of cartons making a place to hang clothes. Apparently, Tinna had rented a furnished place because he could see no major pieces of furniture. Even though he had spent months on end in similar circumstances when he started rebuilding the hacienda, he still wrinkled his nose at the crude living conditions.

Tinna was unloading a stack of used 2x4s from the truck next to the shed. There was already a sizeable pile of used corrugated iron sheets against the wall of the shed.

"Do you want to take a break, or would you like some help unloading?"

"Help unloading. I've got another load to get before dark."

Sage clambered aboard the truck and took one end of the 2x4s so they could toss them down without trying to lift all the weight from one end. As the two fell into a rhythm of chucking the lumber onto the ground, Tinna explained. "As soon as we get the ridge pole up I'll make a roof out of this stuff. It's a little rough, but it's free. I sweet-talked a contractor out of it....if I could get all I needed today. Tomorrow, he'll have the bulldozer shove the building into a pile and haul it away."

When the truck was unloaded, Sage said, "Stop by the house so I can get a pair of gloves and lock the place and I'll go with you."

As they headed for an industrial area northwest of town, Sage told Tinna about the trip and what he'd found out about the secret rooms. They quickly loaded much more than they would need to roof the shed. Tinna said she wanted also to build a shelter over the kiln so it wouldn't deteriorate as quickly.

On the return trip, Tinna hesitated a couple of times, which Sage noticed. He wondered what was on her mind because the blonde Icelander didn't seem to be the type to be cautious about anything. Finally, she got her tongue around the right words.

"I have a proposal." She glanced Sage's way. She noted his raised-brow interest. "Not a proposition, Cabron....a proposal." She forged ahead. "You know that I need a studio and living accommodations. I would like to rent space from you."

Sage drew a breath to say something, but Tinna cut him off. "Let me finish. You've already let me set up my kiln in the brickyard. With a roof and electricity, I can use the shed as a pottery. I have set it up so that I can tap heat from the kiln to warm the pottery in the cold months. Besides, I now have my gas tank there so I can run a gas heater when it is necessary. I'll need water, but I can haul that on the truck.

"As for living, I would like to build living quarters on that raised concrete area on the east side of the granary. I made a sketch. It's in the glove compartment."

Sage pulled out a rough sketch showing a long, narrow construction that ran from the north wall, along the east wall. The measurements showed it to be twelve feet wide and forty-eight feet long. On the north end was a bedroom. A small bath separated the bedroom from the living room, dining area and kitchen, which were all on an open plan.

Tinna pursued her plan. "It wouldn't take much to build one long wall and the short wall on the end. The ceiling would be decked over because there still is eight feet of free space to be used as storage, which is what you're using the space for now.

It wouldn't be hard to heat that small area.

"The reason I'm pushing the idea now is that if you approve, I can make another trip tonight and pick up enough 2x4s to build the walls. And there is a pile of 2x6s that would make the roof. Since I can haul things, I can pick up all the stuff I need for a bath and the kitchen. I can even get the appliances. And I'll pay you the same rent I was paying for the place where I got kicked out."

Tinna stopped talking and glanced at Sage, who was staring straight ahead. Finally, he said, "I've always valued my privacy. Even with all the space in the Hacienda, I never considered taking in a roommate."

"Oh, I wouldn't want to be considered a roommate. I need my private space too, and being a roommate sounds too intimate for me. I just want to be a tenant so I can bitch like a tenant and have the landlord fix the frozen water line."

Sage glanced at the sketch again. It was a pretty good idea. Two walls were already there. The apartment would use the existing windows into the courtyard. He wasn't using the area for anything but storage since most of his heavy construction was over. He also liked the thought of having a regular sum of money coming in. When one depended solely on commissions, one's financial life could get rather hairy. "There is no sewage there. I won't burrow under the wall. The house waste goes into a septic tank with the leech field in the garden area. I suppose I could put in another from the other end. They shouldn't conflict. The water is already there." Sage was primarily talking to himself out loud. Tinna didn't interrupt.

They discussed the possibilities all the way back to the hacienda. As Tinna pulled into the yard, Sage said, "Let's dump the 2x4s behind the granary and go get those 2x6s before it gets too dark."

Sage had two days before he was to return to LA. The first item on the construction agenda was to raise the reinforced concrete beam into the slot for a ridgepole on the shed. Sage had lots of ladders and an assortment of blocks and tackles and rope left over from when he rebuilt the house roof. Tinna's truck had a side-lift winch, which proved to be very helpful.

When Sage headed west in Dreadnought, half of the roof framework was in place. Tinna was cleaning the nails out of more lumber.

It was midmorning when Sage pulled up to the kitchen door of the Brand house. Mrs. Bruckner was pleased to see him, but quickly lapsed into a lethargic state he'd never seen before. She handed him a tray with two cups of coffee and said that Bert was in his office.

Bert was genuinely happy to see a friendly face. "After the murder, it was difficult coping with the horror of it all, but since you left, a different kind of horror walks the land. It all revolves around money and power. The sheriff is getting absolutely nowhere, so he makes life miserable for everyone connected with the case just to make it look like he is doing something. The DA is making political hay out of the lack of progress. The news media is screaming for action and getting all the talking heads in to express baseless opinions.

"Then there are the money hungry vultures trying to pick up whatever they can. Contractors and tradesmen are billing for work never requested. They don't know that I kept track of every transaction Dieter made. He was adamant that there be a paper trail. Then there are the tax people. Everyone seems to think great chunks of Dieter's money is theirs and they want it now.

"On top of that, the kids are raising hell that they didn't split the estate down the middle. Since they aren't instant multimillionaires they are vying for every nickel that is lying around. Karl didn't make it back for the memorial. Elke came looking like a bum and was probably strung out on drugs. Dieter would have had even less respect for his offspring had he been around to see them. Elke has been trying to get into the house probably to clean out anything of value. Since the will was read I haven't let either in. The property doesn't belong to them. I would be more than happy to retrieve any personal property they left behind, but I'm not about to turn them loose in there."

"I'm sorry to hear you've had such a bad time. You'd think people would pull together to help each other get over the loss. Mrs. Bruckner looks like she's really taking it hard."

"She was very fond of Dieter, but the main problem is Immigration. It appears that she will be deported as soon as the sheriff no longer has a need for her. I would say that will pretty much be a death sentence for her. I'll see she always has money, but she has absolutely no desire to return to Germany."

Sage finished his coffee. "I'll bet Mrs. Bruckner will have a lunch ready at noon. I don't want to start putting on the top coat until I have a longer, uninterrupted time period. But I can lay out my material. Can I still use the bedroom upstairs?"

"Sure. Here's the new security code." said Bert, handing Sage a slip of paper. "Don't let the kids know what it is or let them into the house."

Sage looked at the slip and handed it back. "I've got it now."

As Sage passed through the kitchen on the way out to the car to get his luggage, he smiled because the cook was busy getting a big lunch together.

Both Bert and Mrs. Bruckner were busy. Sage set up his halogen lights to flood the end of the room. He had to move some of his stored equipment out of the way. After he started to unscrew the nut on the brass wall light, he thought of the possible fingerprints he had just obliterated. He backed the nut off three-eighths of an inch. He listened for any movement of someone coming his way. When he pushed on the nut, there was a very slight click and a minute movement to the whole, left, ten-foot wall section.

Sage gently pushed against the wall. It easily and soundlessly swung inward revealing about a three-foot space. No finish work had been done. The moveable wall was constructed of exposed studs on the inside on conventional sixteen-inch centers. Exposed concrete blocks with mortar showing were where the windows use to be. Just past the end of the inward swinging door was a gun case with several very expensive shotguns and rifles. There was also a pegboard on the wall with pegs holding a half dozen revolvers and automatics by the trigger guards. There were more pegs than guns. Beyond the gun rack were floor-to-ceiling shelves made out of raw 1x12s. The upper shelves held pieces of expensive looking oriental ceramics, a couple of pieces of carved jade, and a whole group of tiny carved figures an inch or less in size. Against the end wall was a tall stack of cases of ammunition for the various guns in the rack.

Before Sage entered the room he took several photos of the right hand half of the room with his digital camera. In the oblique light from the work lamps, one thing became apparent. The room had never really been cleaned. There was sawdust and general dust on things. Sage shined his light along the floor. There were many marks in the dust, but near the rear of the room one stood out like a beacon. It was a very small barefoot print. It couldn't have been Dieter's. It was very clear along the wall on the office side. The prints showed a high arch with only a slender strip along the outside. The toe prints were very apparent. After taking a picture of it, Sage backed out of the room. Leaving things as they were, he went to Bert's office.

"Hey, Bert, somewhere around here I saw one of those two-inch rolls of transparent tape used for wrapping packages to mail.

"Yeah, there on top of the cabinet."

"Can I borrow it for a bit?"

"Sure, help yourself."

Sage returned to the room and very carefully he stripped off tape and laid two lapped pieces over the footprint. He gently pulled the tape off the floor and transferred it to a page in his sketchbook. He wrote the date and his assumed Chinese name on the page.

Standing in the opening Sage again surveyed the room. Against the end wall that would be the wall between the office and Karl's bedroom was a stack of ammunition boxes about five feet high. They were in front of the built-in shelves. There was a single ammo box on the floor between the stack and the wall to the office. The box sat out from the end wall a few inches. It was just behind where the footprint had been. The urine had come under the wall from a location behind the ammo box.

Sage cast his light on the ammo box, but he could find no sign of anyone urinating on it. But, behind the box there was the yellow ochre stain on the floor. An image began to develop in Sage's mind. A small female had pulled the box far enough away from the wall that she could drape her butt over the ammo box to pee in the corner. It had to be a small female because the box was only about 12 inches wide. Tinna could never wedge her posterior into such a narrow space....by several inches. That would also explain the tiny foot print near the wall with the toes pointing toward the doorway. She had sat on the box. It had to be a female. No male would have done that. He'd have just stood there and shot a stream into the corner.

Hanging on the wall behind the ammo box were several cartridge belts that duck hunters use to carry their extra shells. Velcro tabs replaced buckles. Glistening in the light were some long, strands of yellow hair stuck in the Velcro. Sage backed out of the narrow area. On Dieter's desk there had been a holder with envelopes. Sage appropriated one of the envelopes. Returning to the room, he plucked off one of the hairs. From what he could see with the naked eye, it looked as if it had a follicle still attached. The hair went into the container. He sealed and marked it.

Sage turned around and viewed that half of the secret room from the reverse direction. From that angle he could see the butt of a gun sticking out from between a couple of boxes on a shelf. It didn't appear that there had been an attempt to hide the gun. It was just there. Sage didn't pick up the gun but moved one of the boxes to get a better look. The gun was a Ruger Bearcat. It was a little .22 caliber revolver built on a frontier model frame. *Ah, the murder weapon.* Sage resisted the impulse to touch the gun, even using safeguards to not damage any fingerprints. He was only trying to find out who killed Brand....not convict her. He'd gotten far enough along in his thinking to be able to say "her" with the conviction of knowledge. It was a "her" with long, yellow hair, a narrow ass and tiny feet. Sage took photos of the hair site, the improvised toilet and the gun.

Sage pondered, how did a female get into a hidden room

supposedly only known to Heinz and Brand? Sage doubted that Heinz would have given a potential killer information about the room and how to get into it. Of course, Brand could have told someone, but from what Sage knew, there was no female in his life that would warrant such a confidence.

Either Bert or Mrs. Bruckner could have been told or seen something that would have revealed its presence. Maybe Mrs. Bruckner recognized the shortening of the room. The trip button was cleverly hidden. No one would discover that by accident.

One of the reasons Brand built the room was to keep things out of the grubbing hands of his kids, so he probably wouldn't have confided in them. But, that didn't preclude Elke snooping around. From what Mrs. Bruckner had indicated, she snooped all the time. The sneak had gone through his own personal belongings as soon as she arrived on the scene.

Closing the door as tightly as possible with the lamp cord in the way, Sage took a look at what was behind. That area was where Dieter had stored his expensive wines. There were a few bottles in racks, but most of it was still in cases. Sage could see nothing that seemed connected to the murder case. He had spent more time than he had anticipated in the room, so he quickly closed the door and tightened the nut before Mrs. Bruckner called him to lunch.

Further speculation on what he had found was suspended as he tried to do justice to Mrs. Bruckner's gargantuan lunch. Although it was a rarity, Bert stayed for lunch. He, who normally consumed substantially more than Sage, couldn't put away all the hearty German fare that was stacked on his plate.

While they were eating, Sage guided the conversation to Brand's kids. Now that he didn't have to worry about offending his employer, Bert vented his frustrations with Brand's progeny. They'd had a very proper upbringing with all the amenities wealth could buy. Both youngsters had been excellent students and model citizens until they went to college. About that time, the major stabilizing force in their lives, their mother, died. Apparently, Elke fell under the spell of the pointy-headed, liberal academicians. Brand found that one professor was laying his daughter in broom closets, rest rooms, and any other convenient area where a few moments of privacy could be found. She turned into a false-fronted socialistic anarchist pursuing every ridiculous cause that came along. As long as she could occasionally sneak back home, luxuriate in a bubble bath, and partake of the fruits of wealth, she could play the part of the poverty stricken warrior doing battle with the rich tyrants of our time.

"Karl turned into a lush. The college party scene became his stage. With the money available to him, Karl didn't even have to be enrolled in the college to join its revelers. Karl expanded his horizons to include foreign campuses too. Now that he no longer looks like a college freshman, he's making the transition to the big parties such as Mardi Gras and Cannes."

The front door bell rang. Mrs. Bruckner went to see who was calling. She returned with Lieutenant Fuente. They're still listening. Sage had turned the Global Positioning bug on before he got to LA. It had taken the sheriff less than two hours to send someone around.

"You took off again," said Fuente, accusingly. "You really know how to piss off the sheriff. He wants to have another chat with you."

"I thought you were the lead man on this case. How come he's wasting his valuable time on one he considers to be a poof?"

"Haven't you figured it out yet? He's God and he's going to prove it to you. Come along. We can't keep God waiting."

This time Sage was dressed properly to go out into the public. As they went out the door, Bert called out, "Call me on my cell phone if you need transportation."

Sage sat and sat awaiting the sheriff's pleasure. It took three hours of waiting before the busy man had time for him. Finally, Swain stomped into the interrogation room. Fuente took up his usual position leaning against the wall.

Without preamble, the sheriff stated, "Just before Brand's

murder, you made a $10,000 deposit to your bank account."

I'm going to have to have a word with my bank.

"In view of the circumstances surrounding this murder, we are looking into all questionable financial transactions. How do you account for that deposit?"

"That was not a questionable financial transaction. Besides, that is my personal business and I don't have to answer to you." As Sage was making his statement, he slid his hand onto the tabletop. His index and little finger were extended with the middle and ring fingers and thumb folded under.

Suddenly, Fuente had a coughing fit, which interrupted the sheriff's intended, rage-laden reply. The lieutenant pointed at his throat and gasped, "Tickle," as he headed for the door, still coughing.

Instead of a wide-eye roaring retort, Swain confined himself to a snarling, "Smart ass," as he too left the room.

It was nearly dinnertime before Sage was released. On his own time and in his own car, Fuente drove Sage back to the Brand house. "You're going to get both of us killed. Did you know what you were doing? Do you know what that sign means?"

"Oh, I don't really know who's screwing the sheriff's wife, but it would have been fun if he'd recognized the gesture. He doesn't have much in common with his Hispanic constituents, does he?"

"He considers gays and beaners to be on about the same social level. Both groups will still vote Democratic no matter what he does or says and that's all he cares about."

"Is he still giving Roskal a bad time?"

Fuente laughed. "Not to his face. Roskal has surrounded himself with many attorneys who scream 'harassment' every time the sheriff even looks in his direction. William Pinney is always on the phone to Swain complaining about the attention his client is getting. That doesn't stop the sheriff from assigning an army of investigators who are trying to dig up any dirt they can find. They must have a pretty good database by now."

"Is Pinney Roskal's attorney?"

"There are a lot more, but he is apparently the mouthpiece."

When Sage got to Brand's house, Bert was gone. He let himself in. Mrs. Bruckner must have gone to her room. The kitchen was cold and sterile looking. It seemed to him that outside of Brand, himself, Anna Bruckner was the biggest victim.

The kids didn't seem to care much and they were continuing down their same paths. Bert's life would go on, doing basically the same things. Shortly, Sage would return to his normal routine. But, it was Anna Bruckner who would never go back to anything resembling her old life.

Sage retrieved his cell phone from his luggage and went to Brand's office for a phone book. After finding the number, he dialed Pinney's office. He had expected to get a machine, but instead, he got a real person from an answering service.

After getting the routine about business hours and the like, Sage said, "My name is Sage Grayling. I need to talk with Mr. Pinney, concerning a client of his. We share a common problem named Swain. Please ask him to call me on my cell phone. The Brand house phones may not be safe." Sage gave his number.

As soon as the connection was broken, Sage was sorry he hadn't put some sort of time stipulation on Pinney. It was beyond his dinner time and he was hungry, despite Mrs. Bruckner's lunch. On one of his trips, he'd seen a Mexican restaurant in the vicinity. It took a while to find it, but the Tecate with lemon and salt was worth the effort. He was sopping up the last of the mole sauce with a tortilla when his call came in.

"This is William Pinney. You called?"

"Lieutenant Fuente mentioned you were representing Tony Roskal."

"Yes."

"I need to meet with him, but to do so openly would harden the sheriff's conviction that your client and I are involved in some sort of evil conspiracy."

"Why do you want to meet with Roskal?"

"I need his help in proving neither of us was involved in Brand's murder."

"What do you have?"

"Mr. Pinney, I don't know you and you don't represent me. I'll discuss the matter with Roskal and if he wants to share any information with you, that's his privilege. For now, just please set up the meeting. I have a bug in my car, which I can turn off. But, I wouldn't mind having Tiny set up somewhere so he can see if I'm leading any sort of procession. I don't know much about this area, so you'll have to give me directions. I'm at the Chili Bell on Highland. I'll have a flan and another Tecate while I await your call."

Sage was debating whether to leave or order another beer, when his phone rang. In Arizona he'd have gotten thunderous glares for taking a call at the table, but apparently Californians are more tolerant. It was Pinney with specific instructions. Sage was to turn off the bug and head north on the highway to Exit 98, cross the overhead and return to the Chili Bell. If he was not followed he would be met in the parking lot behind the restaurant. If there was a tail, everything was off for the time being.

On his little excursion, nothing seemed out of the ordinary. When he pulled around the restaurant, the same young, slender man, as on the first meeting with Roskal, was leaning against the fender of a big, black sedan. Sage parked Dreadnought and walked to the sedan. The driver opened the back door. Roskal was seated on the far side of the back seat. This time Sage slid into the car and closed the door.

"Good evening, Mr. Grayling. Tiny says you weren't followed and I had to buy an auto agency to assure myself of a supply of safe cars. You asked to see me."

"Yes, thank you for being so prompt. I have come across something that may get Sheriff Swain off our backs, and I, for one, wouldn't be averse to being able to luxuriate in the sweet taste of revenge."

"What'cha got?" asked Roskal, with a grin. The prospect seemed to please him.

"Let's just say, for the moment, that I have a couple of possible DNA samples. I need your help for several reasons. First, I am a stranger in these parts and I don't know my way around. Secondly, I don't know anything about DNA testing other than what I see on the occasional TV show. And finally, I probably don't have the funds to do it myself. So, what I am asking is that you have one of your attorneys arrange for a lab to examine the specimens to see if they match each other and if they can be matched to a source if I can find one. In short, I have a couple of items that I think came from the killer, but I don't know who the killer is. Oh yes, you pay for the lab work. I'll share the results of the lab work with you. At the moment, I can't tell you where I got the samples. That will have to come after the results are in."

Roskal got crafty. "What makes you think I would get involved in such a vague thing as this? I need a lot more information."

"The carrot I'm holding out is that if I can match these up with a person, I'll give you the pleasure of holding a press conference and announcing to the world that you have done what the sheriff was incapable of doing, solving Dieter Brand's murder. Or would you rather see him as governor of the state? Besides, you once told me 'business is business'."

"I'll talk with Pinney to see what he says."

"Don't talk too long. You set up an appointment for me at a lab and tell me how to get there. I understand there is something called a chain of evidence. I collected the samples. I'll turn them over to the lab and have the lab sign for them. Once we get the returns from the testing, it should lead us in the direction of the killer. Of course, you realize what a leap of faith this is for me. Here I am talking about evidence with the primary suspect in the crime."

"Unless Pinney objects, I'll do it."

"I'd rather you set up another go-between. Swain would immediately connect you and Pinney. Have the new guy call himself Vic. Oh, by the way, how is the real Vic?"

"He's still limping. You're not his favorite person. Vic is now the butt of all the jokes, if you catch my drift. The guys all call him 'Custer'."

"Tell Vic he's a lucky guy. I only had target arrows. The ones with the razor blade hunting tips were in the cabinet he was trying to open. Instead of a 3/8-inch hole, he'd have had one he couldn't cover with a fifty cent piece and it would have nailed him to that ropero."

"Don't keep me waiting too long. I have to get back to Albuquerque."

Back in Dreadnought, Sage turned on the bug again and headed back to Brand's house.

Chapter 8

Roskal didn't waste any time. The pseudo Vic called at 10:00 am to say Sage had an appointment with Dr. Randall at Randall Testing Laboratory at 2:00 that afternoon. Vic also gave instructions on how to get there.

Mrs. Bruckner said that Bert was off on a series of business meetings and would be gone for a few days. Before the appointment, Sage was able to put the final finish on the painting. He was pleased with the finished product. While no one was about, Sage used a pair of channel locks to cinch down the nut on the light fixture so no one would be able to loosen it by hand. During his stay at the house, he'd never seen any tools lying around. There probably were some, but no outsider would know where to look.

By the time he had to leave for his appointment, he had all but the ladders and bars loaded. He'd have to return to pick up the rest of his equipment, and he wanted to say a proper good-bye to Mrs. Bruckner. Without the bug working, he made a quick trip to the lab. The transfer was strictly according to the rules of evidence. Dr. Randall said that he shouldn't expect results to be available for at least a couple of weeks.

Back at the Brand house, Sage finished loading. Mrs. Bruckner was in tears and clung to him a long time in a parting hug. Sage turned on the bug and spent the next two hundred miles in a black funk. Bert had been trying to stop Immigration from deporting Mrs. Bruckner, but he had run into a brick wall. Powerful forces must be operating on the other side. Sage decided that if Bert's efforts didn't pay off, maybe he would facilitate her disappearance. She had lived several decades avoiding the authorities. She shouldn't have any compunctions about doing it again. Sage put those thoughts on hold while he turned his attention to other matters.

He wondered what he would find when he got back to the Hacienda. It appeared Tinna was a very resourceful young woman with considerable useful talents. Not many women could rebuild a classic car. Kiln construction was no small feat either. Also she'd worked right along with him on the shed roof.

When his mind started recalling her physical attributes, Sage put on the clamps. It wouldn't do to introduce a new element into their relationship before the landlord/tenant one had been explored. He had learned that once he took a girl to bed, the rules of the game always changed. He didn't want a bad tenant relationship perpetuated by lust. Of course, a good financial arrangement could also be ruined by a disastrous sexual encounter.

The thought of having someone around the place had grown on him. It would be like having a free house-sitter while he was away. That burglary had shattered his feeling of invulnerability. Having someone to talk to occasionally would be nice too. Another very attractive feature was to have enough money coming in regularly to help pay the monthly bills.

Sage drove around the building. Tinna's truck was not there. But there was a huge pile of construction materials. There was a set of used kitchen cabinets with a stainless steel sink, complete with faucets. A blue commode and lavatory sat off to the side. Sage had to laugh. Included in the pile of materials was a staircase made of heavy stuff

A pass into the brickyard revealed the framework for the pottery roof was up and some of the corrugated metal was in place. The kiln was not belching heat. Tinna's truck wasn't there either.

Sage pulled into his garage and began unloading the rack on top of Dreadnought. As he was levering the last ladder onto its hanger, Tinna's truck came rolling down the lane. When she saw the garage door open, she hit the horn but pulled around to the other side of the house.

Their paths met in the kitchen. "Welcome back," said Tinna with a grin.

"I'm always glad to be back. I need a cup of coffee....you?"

"Sure. Did you finish the painting or just come up with another body?"

"The painting is all finished and paid for, and I picked up a note for the down payment on the Texas painting. Luke will actually write that check out at his end of the empire. It looks as if you've been busy. That's quite a pile of materials out back. How did you come up with all that?"

"Oh, you just have to know which day to hit which district. It's amazing what Americans throw away. All that stuff was left out on the curb for the garbage truck. We would never be so wasteful in Iceland. I've got an electric range, refrigerator and a washer and drier in the granary. They're all supposed to work."

"I have a week or so before I have to leave for Texas. The lab reports may change that. In any case we should be able to get some construction work done."

As Tinna accepted her cup of Nescafe, she said, "What lab report? You sick?" She looked at him a little warily.

"No. Not that kind of lab. I'll tell you about it later in the order of things."

"Are you still a murder suspect?" said Tinna, as she returned to her original train of thought.

"The sheriff still thinks I am. That bastard has been snooping in my financial matters. He had me in the office for another little session. I'm going to have a few words with my bank. Come on, I've got to get on the computer. I think I can prove the murderer was a female."

"Female?"

"I found the source of the yellow stain. It came from inside the secret room and ran under the wall. And there's a lot more." Sage transferred the digital camera images into the computer. As he brought the various shots onto the screen, he explained what they were looking at. He queued the photos into his printer. As the prints were coming out, Sage related what he had found and what he had done. He pulled his sketch book out of his luggage to take the first, good look at the bare footprint he had lifted with the tape. There was an amazing amount of detail, but at first he didn't know what he was seeing. It was Tinna who pointed out the texture that showed heavy callusing with cracks instead of normal skin.

"That chick doesn't wear shoes."

"That should limit the field of suspects considerably," said Sage. "Of course, in California anything can happen. Maybe they outlawed shoes in San Francisco and I just missed the announcement."

"What are you going to do with this stuff?"

"The urine sample and the hair strand are in a DNA lab being analyzed to see if they match. I'll wait to see what the lab has to say. If they can read the DNA, then we should be able to make a positive identification of who was in that room. I would think the gun will give even more evidence. Of course, it will be up to the DA to prove all of it in a court. That may be a problem in California. Guilt doesn't mean anything there."

Sage decided not to spend much of his time pondering the murder because he wanted to concentrate on getting a good portion of the apartment built before he had to leave town again.. He and Tinna put in long hours doing carpentry work. Sage refined Tinna's sketch of the apartment, putting it into standard US dimensions. Tinna had already removed all the nails from the scavenged lumber, so Sage jigged up the radial arm saw to cut the ceiling and studs to proper length. They marked out the plan on the concrete slab. When the various plumbing fixtures were located, holes were chiseled in the cement and pipes were laid.

One morning, Sage started nailing the wall units together. Tinna headed out to scavenge doors and windows. Later in the day, the pair had a raising party. All the stud walls were lifted into place and bolted to the concrete. Braces kept them upright until the joists could tie them together.

It had been a good day's work. Sage noted that Tinna had kept pace with him all day. Within his experience, no woman had ever stayed with him in such a prolonged physical endeavor.

When they finally decided to break for the day, Tinna said she would take care of dinner. She'd stopped at the market while she had been scrounging doors. Before mixing martinis, Sage announced he had to clean up first. Tinna wanted to get the potatoes on to boil. Sage was just building a lather in the shower when Tinna came thumping in from the jardin. She sat down on a commode to pull off her boots. Then she tossed her clothes over a stanchion and took the shower at the other end of the line. "Don't pig all the hot water."

"Hog," corrected Sage. "With the size of the hot water tank I put in, that's not a problem," Sage replied, as he was losing the battle of trying to maintain an air of indifference to the naked lady a few feet away. But, he'd be damned if he was going to turn away, so she remained in his peripheral vision. When he caught her inspecting him, she merely smiled and said, "We don't see many peeled onions in Iceland."

"Peeled onions?"

"Circumcisions." Tinna turned to rinse the shampoo out of her hair as Sage scowled at his unruly peeled onion. Tinna stripped the water out of her hair as she stepped to the cupboard for towels. One she wrapped around her hair. She tossed one to Sage as he turned off the shower. The third she used to dry herself. Tossing the wet towel into the hamper beside the washer, she collected her clothes and shoved her feet into her cowboy boots before heading out through the dirt back yard to her make-shift room. "I'll be back before the potatoes are done."

If he was going to maintain an unencumbered relationship with that gorgeous body, Sage was going to have to do a lot of plumbing in a hurry. There was a lot of uncertainty in how long he could be good with Tinna taking a shower right next to him.

Before he could get everything under control, he heard the potter rustling around in the kitchen. After Sage got presentable, he went to the kitchen where Tinna was merrily halving a roasted chicken. She had changed into a very stretchy tube top, short shorts, and sandals. That was the first time he'd ever seen her in any foot gear other than cowboy boots. She was still showing an awful lot of skin, which was not helping his resolve one bit.

As the construction work progressed, they fell into a comfortable routine of working until about 6:00. Cleanup became less harrowing. After a martini, one or the other would cook. Post-dinner coffee was taken in the sitting area of his bedroom. This more relaxed arrangement was facilitated by Sage confronting the issue of intimacy with Tinna. They decided on a working relationship that, for the time being, circumvented sex.

Sage was enough of an electrician that he would handle that end of the job. He had some materials left over from his earlier wiring projects. Tinna was able to come up with more wire. Sage had to buy a few fixtures. The big expense was the plywood. They could hide used 2x4s, but used sheeting would show. They were able to scrounge some heavy plywood for the roof/floor of the second level. The rest Sage had to purchase.

Although most of the finish work had to be done, Tinna had an enclosed area to call home. Sage was beginning to think about Texas. One evening, they were drinking coffee and watching an evening news broadcast, when Sage bolted upright. He dove for the Tivo recorder. The story on the TV concerned an environmental demonstration that was being held in a black-tailed prairie dog city just outside of Dallas, Texas. The leader of the protest was a woman who called herself Caliwildflower. She had come to fame for the two years she had sat in an ancient, gnarled cypress tree that clung to a cliff over a tiny inlet of the Pacific Ocean. Sage remembered the news reports. The high rocks on the seaward side of the inlet protected the tree from the Pacific storms. There had been a whole army of sympathizers to haul food up and to carry away waste. She was protesting the destruction of venerable old trees that were located in the path of civilized expansion.

Now, she was building a two-foot high tent maze on the edge of a black-tailed prairie dog city on the outskirts of Dallas. By keeping a low silhouette, she hoped to be accepted by the black-tails as a member of their community. The land in question was slated to be developed for a strip mall and to be surrounded by housing. Caliwildflower was planning on inhabiting the land in the same way as she had the tree in California. She and her sympathizers hoped to disrupt the sale to a developer in hopes of protecting the prairie dog city. There were some file pictures of Caliwildflower as well as current footage of her crawling around under a low tent and peering out at prairie dogs.

It wasn't until the bit was finished that Tinna said, "What's all that about?"

"That's the girl that was with Elke Brand at the house when Elke smeared the peace sign on my painting. I had forgotten all about her. All I saw of her was her face as she looked around the bedroom door. Her hair was wrapped in a towel. Look how tiny she is. She's got long yellow, blonde hair and in that picture she was bare-footed. She'd match the physical description I have in mind for the occupant of that secret room. She was in the house a few days before the murder. And, as far as I can tell, whoever was in that room didn't get the information about the room from anyone who was supposed to know....Heinz or Brand. So, someone had to find it and the only one with such an opportunity would be Mrs. Bruckner, Bert or Elke. I have no reason to suspect either of the first two. But Elke is known for her snooping. She may have found out about the room and I think it was her friend that killed Brand. I don't know why that Cali woman would do it, but I'm going to proceed with the assumption she did."

Sage moved over to the computer. For the next couple of hours he searched the internet archives of newspapers and magazines as well as websites that dealt with Caliwildflower's type of protests. He located her real name...Elizabeth Wren. In more recent times, her real name disappeared as she became better known as Caliwildflower. There were numerous photos of her. He copied a couple of shots.

It was still early enough to call Bert at home, who reported there was still no progress to report on the murder. Another battle was raging with the sheriff who wanted to rummage around in Brand's financial records to look for suspects. Bert strongly suspected he was really selling access to competitors.

When Sage put the question to him about the girl with Elke, he confirmed she was the tree-sitter, but he couldn't think of her name at that moment. She was a frequent visitor to the house. However, there were several other girls whom Elke would drag in. It was Bert's opinion that none of them were worth a pound of dog doodoo.

"Bert, outside of the tree-sitter, can you remember any other girls who would be about the same size, blonde and bare-footed?"

After a few moments of thought, Bert said that he could think of none, but then Elke's friends were the kind one liked to quickly forget.

Sage pressed on. "The cleaning maids came the morning of the murder. Can you remember if they had been there since Elke and her tree-sitter were there?"

"Let me look at my calendar. Those are the kind of things I jot down. I have to pay the cleaning service. Also I record the comings and goings of the kids in case something comes up at a later date." There was a brief delay. "No, the cleaners weren't here in between those two dates. Why?"

"I'll tell you when I get there. I'm leaving here as soon as I can get my things together. I'll give you a call when I can give you an arrival time. In the interim, don't let anyone into the house. I have something to show you and I don't want it disturbed. Is

Mrs. Bruckner still there?"

"Yes."

"She may be in danger. It might be worth the expense to put a guard on the house. She probably couldn't repel a determined intruder."

"You know something."

"Well, I think I do, but under the circumstances I'd rather tell you directly."

When Sage turned back to Tinna, he said, "I'm sorry, but the construction will have to be delayed a bit. This will probably take a few days to settle. I'll leave now and stop when I get tired.

*****

Sage had called ahead, so Bert was waiting for him at the house. Sage had timed his arrival to get there in the morning. An armed guard blocked his way until he identified himself. Mrs. Bruckner was looking even worse than before. Sage really felt sympathy for her as she gave him a tray of coffee to take to Bert's office.

As Sage's story unfolded, he watched closely for any sign that Bert might already know about the room. But Bert's reaction convinced Sage that there was no prior knowledge. Bert wanted to see the room right away.

"I think you'd better wait until you hear the rest of the story." Sage continued with his narrative, laying out his thinking along the way. "What I want to do first is go to the master bedroom to see if we can find anything that will give us a sample of DNA from Caliwildflower. When I saw her, I think she had just washed her hair....probably taken a shower. I'd like to see if there might be another hair sample around the bathroom.

"There probably will be. Those girls always leave a horrible mess. The best place to start would be the hair bush. There is complete set of grooming devises that Mrs. Brand used. They are still on her dressing table. Dieter would never touch them."

Bert was right. One of the hair brushes was loaded with snarls of yellow blonde hair. With a pair of tweezers, Sage pulled out a hair with a follicle attached. That went into an envelope, which was sealed and marked. On his cell phone, Sage called the Randall DNA lab. It took time to get through to Dr. Randall. After he identified himself, he inquired as to the progress of the samples that had been submitted earlier.

"The testing has been done and we are currently completing the evaluation. I'm not sure of the exact stage, but I'd guess that in three or four days, the results will be final."

"Doctor, I have another hair sample. This time it is from another location. If I bring it down, could you check it against what you have?"

"Certainly, but that will take time, just like the first sample. There will be an additional charge for the work."

"Understood. I'll have authorization called in before I bring over the new sample. Thank you, doctor."

Sage's next call was to Pinney, Roskal's attorney. Sage finally made it as far up the ladder as the Executive Assistant-something-or-other. Sage identified himself and tried to explain what he needed, without getting too explicit, along with the urgency of the situation. But he couldn't get any commitment of any kind....even on a simple call-back. Mr. Pinney was such a busy man.

Egotistical, elitist asshole! Sage punched the off button in disgust. "Do you have any idea how I can get in touch with Roskal?"

"I have the number of the longshoreman's union. We were dealing with them on the port facility. They should know where he is, providing they'll tell you."

When Sage got through to the union hall, he didn't ask for Roskal. He told the receptionist, "I need Tiny's cell number."

"Tiny, who?"

"Tiny, who? Man-mountain Tiny. That Tiny. The boss's.... shall we say, associate."

"Oh, Tiny."

"Yeah, that Tiny....the number?"

The receptionist rattled off the number from memory. "Thanks."

Bert laughed. "I'm glad I don't have to go against you. You're devious."

Sage dialed. "Tiny, do you remember the guy with the funny looking old Caddy?....Right. I need to talk to the boss right away. He'll think it's important....Good."

Sage smiled benignly at Bert as he waited for Tiny to get to the boss.

"Mr. Roskal, Sage here. I need you to call the lab and authorize another test. I think I may have found a known match for the unknown samples. If that's the case, then, in a few days, you will have what you need to make that announcement we were discussing."

"You know, you're gettin' expensive."

"Me? You haven't paid me a nickel. For that matter, I suspect none of this is coming out of your pocket. If it is, you're not crafty enough to hold down that job. If you want to save money, dump Pinney. He's not tending to your business. I'll be at the lab at 2:00." Sage hung up without explaining his Pinney comment. It will be more fun this way.

Turning to Bert, he said, "How do you get in touch with Elke, when it's necessary?"

"That's not easy to do. She doesn't file any flight plan. Why?"

"I'm toying with an idea. I may want to send her a picture. The other day, when I called, I had just seen Caliwildflower on TV protesting about the development over a prairie dog city. I didn't see Elke on TV. Do you know if she was there?"

"I have no idea, but I can call Luke to see if he knows something."

"Good. In the interim, I need a computer with Photoshop, a

scanner and a printer."

"Dieter's computer is the latest thing. I doubt if he has that program, but I'm sure someone in the organization has it. I can get it loaded by the time you get back from the lab."

Chapter 9

—m—

It was getting late in the afternoon before Sage got back. He had stopped to make some purchases.

Bert reported that he had called Texas. "Luke thought Elke was around somewhere. That demonstration you saw over TV was on a chunk of Dieter's property that Luke has been negotiating to sell to a real estate developer. Dieter bought the land for the commercial site along the highway. He'd made his money by developing the front section. He wasn't interested in doing the residential work. Remember when the kids found out that they hadn't inherited all the estate? Luke thinks the kids had a side deal that Elke would take all the Texas property and Karl the California property. Elke told Luke not long ago he'd never be able to sell that land. She was going to preserve it as a prairie dog city. Luke didn't pay too much attention because she was always saying wild things like that."

Mrs. Bruckner broke up their conversation by announcing dinner. Bert declined, saying his wife was expecting him. It turned into a rather strained dinner. Sage couldn't get any conversation from Mrs. Bruckner beyond simple yeses and nos. She wouldn't sit down to eat or even drink a cup of coffee. She just shuffled

128

about the kitchen going through unnecessary functions. She wouldn't talk about herself at all.

After dinner, Sage took a cup and carafe of coffee up to Dieter's office. As Bert had indicated, his computer was a real charger. There was the latest scanner and printer too. The most recent version of Photoshop was loaded.

Sage started his project by setting up his purchase from a local pet store. It was a small, wire animal cage with an exercise wheel in it. He took a digital photo of it. A search of the house produced a relatively recent photo of Elke. He retrieved, from his luggage, the photo of Caliwildflower he'd downloaded from the net.

With all of his bits and pieces in hand, he began scanning and manipulating photos. It was well into the night before he printed off a composite photo.

He had produced two rodent cages. From the book he had purchased, he made a pair of black-tailed prairie dogs, giving each one of the girls' faces. Elke's had her dark hair and Caliwildflower had yellow hair. The rodents were running on exercise wheels in cages. The cages were on paths that swept around and went toward vanishing points. Periodically, decade road signs were posted. After 50 they were too small to read. The sheet was titled MURDER ONE. When he was satisfied with his work, he saved one version into JPEG so he could send it over the internet.

In the morning, Sage showed Bert the secret room. He wouldn't let Bert go in, because it was a crime scene. Neither wanted to contaminate it any further or give Swain any cause to give Bert grief.

Bert got a good laugh out of Sage's late-night computer efforts. He produced Luke's e-mail address and while Sage was sending the print, Bert got Luke on the phone to tell him to expect the photo and print it on photo paper so it would show at its best. Then Luke was to have an anonymous delivery agent get the print to Elke. Luke was told to deny any knowledge of the photo in case Elke came asking.

Bert had to go off on appointments, leaving Sage to his own

devices. The only thing left for Sage was to erase all traces of his computer work. It involved more than simple deletions. He had to get into the memory and history files not only where he had built the composite but where he'd sent it to Luke. That involved a lot of work, but Sage welcomed it, because the whole program was now on hold until other things took place. He had time to realize just how far out on the horns of speculation he actually was. In his own mind, he felt certain his scenarios were correct, but there was no evidence to back them up....yet. He hadn't even gotten the results back from the first DNA tests when he was trying to match them with a new sample. He was surmising that the gun would point toward the prairie dog lover. He was also assuming that those hair and urine samples were hers. The same was true of the footprint. It all looked good, but as of the moment, there was no proof.

Then he had gone further out on the limb to send Elke the photo. If the situation was as Sage was presuming, Elke would realize that someone had made the connection between her and the murderer. However, making the connection and proving it were entirely different things. With that connection having been made, the existence of the physical evidence in the secret room could not wait for a convenient time to clean things up. She had originally been cleared of any suspicion because she was in another state at the time. The troubling thing would be trying to figure out who had made the connection between the two of them. The sheriff wouldn't employ such a tactic. She would probably eliminate Bert and Luke, unless she felt they might be trying to blackmail her, but she didn't have any money and they controlled millions of dollars that should have been hers. Because of their run-in, Sage's name might cross her mind. He was working on the wall and he might have stumbled onto the secret room. If so, why would he not tell the sheriff? Blackmail? There were other scenarios, but no matter which one it was, she had to destroy the evidence. Sage's operating hypothesis was that Elke and probably Caliwildflower would beat a hot path to California and try to gain entry to the room to remove the gun. She wouldn't know about his already finding the room. Also it wasn't in Sage's scheme to expose the existence of the room until he was ready to use that information to fulfill his plan.

Sage figured he could relax until the following night. It would take Elke that long to get to California. After that, he'd have to be on his toes. His job would be to keep her in town but out of the house. He passed the evening using Brand's search engine to poke around the internet in areas of interest.

In the interim, the only diversion that appealed to him was to pull Swain's tail. In the morning, Sage tried to cheer up Mrs. Bruckner, but to no avail. She went about her chores mechanically. Being with her reminded him of a TV special he'd seen recently about Death Row.

After breakfast, he escaped in Dreadnought. He turned on the bug and headed toward the Sheriff's Office. He already knew the sheriff wouldn't be in because of an announcement on the morning news that reported the sheriff would be attending a civic function. Since they didn't have a "suspects' parking lot," Sage had to settle for "visitors."

At the front desk, he asked to see Sheriff Swain. The receptionist said the sheriff was out of the office and he was not expected back until after lunch.

"May I have a piece of paper? I would like to leave a note for him."

In his most elegant Spenserian script, using his own flexible-nib fountain pen, he wrote: "Most Honorable Harvey Lawrence Swain, Since there has been no movement toward finding the murderer of Dieter Brand, I feel it is my civic duty to offer my assistance. Please, do not hesitate to call upon me for any service I can provide." Sage signed it, "Sincerely, Sage Grayling, Trompe L'Oeil Artist. PS. Happy Birthday next Thursday. SG."

Sage had picked up the sheriff's middle name and birthday off the internet. With a broad smile, he slid the sheet to the receptionist without folding it. It was open for anyone to read.

On the way out the door he ran into Lieutenant Fuente.

"What are you doing here?" demanded the lieutenant.

"Since Swain hasn't made any arrests in the Brand case, I

stopped by to offer my assistance. The sheriff is not in, so I left him a note to that effect." Sage nodded back to the reception desk where a knot of people were hovering over the hapless receptionist.

Fuente rolled his eyes upward. "I still think you have a death wish. What are you doing back in town? You were safe in Albuquerque."

"There's no fun in being safe. Besides, I have a strong sense of honor, which must be defended at all cost. By the way, how is the sheriff taking his failure?"

"Not well. Because it was such a high profile case, he injected himself directly into the initial investigation, hoping to garner some much needed publicity. Now that the case has stalled, he is beginning to get a lot of adverse publicity, which makes him dangerous."

"Are you feeling the heat?"

Fuente glanced around to see if there was anyone close by. "Life around him is usually miserable, but this case is making him even more of a chingón. Watch out. As soon as he finds out you're back in town he'll probably take out his frustrations on you. You'd be wise to put some miles between you and LA."

"Thanks for the warning, but he's already lost the game, except he doesn't know it yet. Anything he does now will only dig him a deeper political grave. The game never was the murder, but the governorship."

The lieutenant's eyes narrowed as he listened to Sage. "Is there something I should know?"

"No, not from me. There are other forces that are beginning to stir. When they fully awaken, the future will become much clearer. Stay nimble so you don't get caught in the cross-fire."

"What the hell are you talking about? What do you know that I don't?" demanded Fuente.

"I don't know anything for sure. I'm a little psychic. I feel things."

"Ah, bullshit. You must be eating peyote." Fuente mouthed the words, but his base Mexican belief in the supernatural peeked through. "I still think you'd be wise to get out of town."

Considering Swain's predilection to make enemies suffer, Fuente's advice probably should have been taken. As Sage drove back to the Brand house, he bounced the alternatives around in his mind. He felt relatively certain Elke was probably on her way to California. If that had not been the case, Sage might have been tempted to take a tour up the coast until the DNA work was complete. However, Elke and Caliwildflower constituted a sufficient threat that he wanted to be available. He'd already been an object of one of Elke's unprovoked attacks. Sage didn't want to subject Mrs. Bruckner to such a possibility. He decided that in the morning he'd ask Bert to get the guards back.

Mrs. Bruckner prepared a hearty dinner for Sage. He had to eat alone because the cook said she wasn't hungry and didn't feel like talking. His dinner companion turned out to be a book from the family library.

Before securing the house, he got a door opener from Mrs. Bruckner and moved Dreadnought into one of the garages. There were three empty bays. The garage was detached and set a ways behind the house. Since there were no windows, neither the sheriff nor Elke should be able to spot it. Returning to the house, he gave Mrs. Bruckner direct orders not to open the door to anyone. He would take care of any callers. He asked her to stay in her room if someone came. Sage set the alarm system and retired to his room.

Sometime in the middle of the night something woke Sage. He couldn't tell what time it was because he didn't have his big digital alarm clock that sat beside his bed at home. He listened intently for a bit, but nothing else caused any concern. He dropped off to sleep again. That sleep was shattered when the fire alarm began its raucous clamor. He could hear and see nothing. The draperies were pulled and the door was shut. When he opened the door, the smell of smoke was evident. A faint light came up the stairs from the night light in the entry hall. Sage bounded down the stairs. He flipped on the light in the entry. Smoke was coming from the rear of the house. He checked the front parlor, but it was clear. Going down the entry to the rear parlor he spotted smoke coming from under the door. He tested the door knob. It was warm but not hot. Opening the door he saw a puddle of flame on the floor along the outer, rear wall. He also smelled gasoline. The flames had already taken the curtain from the windows and were licking at the ceiling. A davenport was engulfed in flame. All the doors to the room were shut, so Sage closed the one into the hall to cut off air. He ran to the kitchen for the phone and to get Mrs. Bruckner out of her quarters. As he reached for the phone, it rang. When he grabbed the receiver as voice said, "This is the security company. We are recording a fire...."

"Right," said Sage. "Get the Fire Department rolling. It is in the rear parlor. There is one other person in the house and I'm getting her out now." Sage dropped the phone so it dangled on its cord as he started shouting "Anna, Anna, Anna."

Sage grabbed the door knob to her quarters. It was locked. He backed off a bit and hit the panel in the middle of the door with his shoulder. It collapsed inward. He changed to "Fire, Fire, Fire." By the time he got into the sitting room, Mrs. Bruckner was coming out the door to her bedroom. She had her robe in her hand.

"There's a fire in the back parlor. Are there any fire extinguishers in the house?"

"In the closet by the refrigerator. There's another big one in the basement. I'll get it." Mrs. Bruckner darted out the side door of the kitchen before Sage could object. She was no longer an old, lethargic women waiting to die.

Sage ran back to the parlor. The door knob was getting hotter. He thrust the door open and began spraying the powdered chemical. He couldn't get very close to the flames because again he wasn't wearing anything. By the time the canister was empty, Mrs. Bruckner was back with a much larger foam thrower. In German, she yelled, "There's a hose on the porch."

It took a moment for the words to sink in before he launched himself down the hall to the side door. The hundred feet of garden hose easily reached the parlor. As he started spraying water on the wall and ceiling he realized the reason for the fire. The secret room was directly above. With renewed effort he hosed down the fire.

He could hear the sirens in the distance. "Open the front door," he yelled at Mrs. Bruckner. Sage wasn't putting the fire out, but he was keeping it from really getting out of control. He was down on his knee to get below the dense smoke still putting water on the fire, when he was relieved by the first fireman. Sage withdrew with a fit of coughing.

As soon as he could breathe again he raced upstairs. He first checked the office. The electricity was still on. The door to the secret room was still closed. He stood for several seconds watching around the edges of the door to see if any smoke was coming out. He went into Karl's old room. The floor was hot, but he could see no signs of the fire coming through the floor. His room was further forward than the fire. Outside of smoke that hung in the hall and some that had drifted into the room, everything was all right. He used the opportunity to get dressed.

By the time Sage got back to the ground floor, the fire was out. He told the firemen he'd checked upstairs and there didn't seem to be any damage. They didn't believe him. A couple of men went up. Sage was a little antsy until they tromped back down saying everything was all right.

Sage didn't know fire department ranks, but the one who was obviously in charge said he had some questions to ask. Sage suggested they talk in the kitchen where he hoped Mrs. Bruckner was brewing coffee. He was right. He asked her to call Bert.

However, the fireman didn't want to talk before Mrs. Bruckner. He led the way to the dining room. He introduced himself as Captain Walter Finch. After the preliminaries....name, age, address and other related facts, Finch started asking leading questions into the start of the fire to which Sage said, "I think you'll find out this is arson."

"What makes you think that?"

"When I opened the door, there was a puddle of fire on the floor and I could smell gasoline."

"Well, we're working on that assumption until we can be proven wrong. The arson squad is on its way. It would appear someone cut a circle out of the high window in that room. There was obviously an accelerant used. I understand you were in the house when a murder was committed. So who did it?"

"Did which?"

"Either or both. What do you think are the chances that the two incidents are related?"

"I'd say they were probably pretty good."

"Now that the owner is dead, whose house is this?"

"It belongs to the estate. There is a trust so Brand's charitable work can continue."

"As I recall, there were a couple of kids....and they didn't get the property?

"Right. They weren't too happy about it from what I hear."

"Would either of them burn down the house?"

"Probably either of them could, but I hear the son is at a big party in Europe and the last I heard, the daughter was in Texas."

Mrs.Buckner brought in two cups of coffee and announced that Bert had just arrived.

Sage told Finch about Bert and his position with the estate.

When Finch said he needed to get some information from Bert, Sage asked if he could go upstairs to see if his painting had been damaged. As Sage started up the stairs, he heard his name called. It was Lieutenant Fuente.

"What brings you out at this hour of the night?" said Sage.

"The immediate cause was Sheriff Swain. He got word of the fire here and sent me to find out what type of coincidence would cause a murder and an arson to occur in the same house so close together."

"Does he think I set the fire?"

"If he can't pin the murder on you, he might settle for arson."

"Great."

"What does your second sight have to say about this new state of affairs?"

Sage smiled slightly, "The stirring seems to be accelerating, doesn't it?"

"Where were you going when I came in?"

"I was going to open the doors to get the smoke out of my room."

"Do you suppose this fire could have been set by the murderer to destroy evidence?

"That thought crossed my mind," said Sage, "but you guys made a thorough sweep. You scooped up everything....and tried to ruin everything you couldn't carry away. There couldn't be much left.

"There's one area where we couldn't look."

Sage hoped his involuntary tensing hadn't showed. "Where was that?"

"Mills got a court order to keep us out of the computers. There may be some incriminating evidence there that would be worth destroying."

"I don't much wonder why Swain lost that one. If he was a straight shooter he might have gotten to take a look, but the word is out that he'd pinch any sensitive info and sell it to the competition....anything to get votes. As far as I know, there's nothing in Brand's computer any more. It has been backed up and the files purged. I was using it to surf the internet last night and there weren't any files in there. But, probably the arsonist wouldn't have known that. Also there is a computer at Brand's downtown office. I would suppose that one had the same stuff. When Brand was killed there was an external hard drive sitting on the desk. I don't remember seeing it last night. Maybe Bert took it. In any case, the murderer could have picked up the hard driver or the computer the night he killed Brand."

"There was some reason for setting that fire. Tomorrow, the sheriff is going to send a forensic team to take another look."

"If he messes up my painting again, he will get sued," declared Sage angrily. "Anyone who touches it will be included. I repaired it at my own expense the first time, but not again." Sage stomped up the stairs with a stiff back. Fuente didn't follow. Sage slammed the door to his room and waited to see if there was any activity outside. Just in case Fuente decided to come up, Sage opened the sliding doors to the balcony.

There was a lot of activity below on the lawn. Sage stayed in the shadows to listen. Apparently the arson squad had arrived, because Finch was telling a new man what had been found. In the flower border a little further toward the back of the house.... several little wires with flags marked something. From his vantage point he could see a disk of glass in the flowers. Finch was saying, "This is an old house. It's just single strength. Easy to cut. The cut was made so it wouldn't break any of the alarm strips. Also, it wasn't made so one could reach the latch. I'd say it was cut just to pour the accelerant in. The arsonist took the empty container away."

"Do you have any theories on why this window was chosen?

"There could be any number of reasons. It's the darkest area. There is a live-in cook who has an apartment on the other side. The fire would have been well established before she would have been affected if it hadn't been for the alarm company. There was a house guest upstairs, but not too many would have known that."

"It's still strange that he cut a hole avoiding an alarm system and was thwarted by the same alarm system," said the arson man.

"It might have gotten out of control before the truck could have gotten here, but the guest and the cook put two extinguishers on the flames and used a garden hose before help got here. Let me show you the inside."

Sage backed into his room, wrinkling his nose at the acrid smell in the air. He propped his door open. He felt the floor over the fire. It was slightly warm to the touch. In the office he made a quick check of the painting. There was a little smoke staining on the very light areas. There was enough there that he could make a fuss about having to spend the time cleaning it. He made the rounds through Brand's small office, bath and bedroom, leaving all the doors open so they could air out. Before leaving he turned out all the lights.

Bert had finished answering questions. He was in his office. When Sage showed up, Bert said, "Would you go help Mrs. Bruckner? Her English is failing her again. The fire investigator needs to ask her a few questions."

Mrs. Bruckner was a little heap on a chair at the breakfast table. She was still in her robe. The fireman was apparently waiting for Sage. "Mr. Mills says you can speak German. Could you help me out?"

Sage settled down next to Mrs. Bruckner and softly said, "Someone tried to burn the house down and the fireman are trying to find out who did it. They need to know if you saw or heard anything that would help."

For the next twenty minutes Sage got absolutely no helpful information from the cook. She hadn't seen or heard anything out of the ordinary. She had been awakened by the alarm and Sage had broken in her door to get to her.

The firemen were cleaning up when Sage went back to Bert's office. The entry and the parlor were disaster areas, but the rest of the house had not suffered too much. Bert would have to hire a service for fire and water damage. Bert had called the security company and a couple of guards were being dispatched to watch over the house until further notice.

When everyone had left and Mrs. Bruckner had been sent off to bed again, Sage and Bert settled down with an early morning brandy. "Who do you think started the fire?" asked Bert.

"I rather suspect they are both here. The sheriff could probably find out from the airlines, but that can wait. I'll also bet they watched the whole operation from the hills above here. Elke probably used to roam those hills as a kid. And her friend is a nature lover. They parked a rental car somewhere on the other side and walked in. That fire took off so fast, the arsonist couldn't have gotten away very far before the alarm went off. They may still be out there."

"They wouldn't have known you were staying here. Anna said you'd parked your car in the garage. Do you think they'll try again?"

"It will be more difficult with the guards here. By the way, Swain is sending a forensic team back tomorrow because he thinks the fire was started to destroy evidence the murderer must have left behind. The current thinking is that there must be some implicating information on Brand's computer. Since you blocked their rummaging through the computer files, they think they missed something."

"They won't find anything. I backed up everything and then put in a new hard drive. I reloaded the programs. There is nothing there."

"I told Fuente I'd surfed the internet last night and I didn't see any files there. I also told the lieutenant that probably the murderer wouldn't know the files were gone. Anyway, be prepared for a tedious day in a few hours. I'm going to try getting a little sleep before I have to confront Swain or his minions."

Chapter 10

—⟨⟨⟨⟩⟩⟩—

Sage made no pretense of getting up until it was necessary. At 9:00 am he had to, because a fleet of forensic people descended on the house. A bleary-eyed Fuente was in charge. Sage refused to talk to anyone until he had coffee and breakfast. Fuente joined him. Mrs. Bruckner laid out her usual old-world spread. This time, the forensic team was poking into everything....even the basement that Sage hadn't known existed until Mrs. Bruckner went there to get the big fire extinguisher. Sage excused himself to go to the bathroom. While he was upstairs, he poked his head into the office. He interrupted a couple of techs ethernetting the contents of Brand's computer hard drive into a laptop.

Both men jumped when Sage said, "That's a direct violation of a court order."

One of them stammered, "We....we didn't know that."

"Tell Swain, that breaking the law isn't going to net him anything. That's a new hard drive in there. There's nothing there to sell." Sage turned on his heel and went back down to Fuente.

"What new surprises has Swain in store for me today?"

"Nothing new. We're supposed to go over every inch of this house to find out why someone would want to burn it down. Then I'm to take you down town for another interview with the sheriff, but this time there won't be any news media around to whom you can make inflammatory remarks. He didn't appreciate that note you left for everyone to see."

"Since the public has already heard my inflammatory remarks, you tell the sheriff that if he wants to interview me, there had better be an independent, third party witness or preferably my attorney present....of course, I can't afford an attorney....or I'll have my own little press conference to report that I was held incommunicado. And that it was my opinion that it was because he wanted me to service him. And I'll say I want to make it clear that I don't swing that way."

"Boy, you really know how to dig a hole for yourself. Don't you realize you are out of your territory and the sheriff can make life absolutely miserable for you and you can't do a thing about it?

"Who says I can't do anything about it? He can harass me and waste my time and money, but he can't put me in jail unless he manufactures evidence that I did something wrong. Then he's the criminal and not me. He may be a big fish in this pond, but to me this pond is only a wet spot. I can still get all the work I can handle even if I never come back to this county or this state again."

"Well, don't underestimate the misery he can cause. I've got to go see how the boys are doing. As soon as they're finished, I'm to take you down to visit with the man."

Sage had another cup of coffee while he sweated out whether the forensic techs would stumble onto the secret room. The end result would probably be the same in that the murderer would be exposed and prosecuted, but an unprincipled bastard would get the credit and use that credit to his own political advantage. If Swain ever became the governor of California, the whole state would suffer.

Mrs. Bruckner had retreated to her room, leaving him with nothing to do. Since Bert had not shown up, Sage suspected he was ducking the sheriff. Sage called the Mills house and got the Mrs. After she identified who was calling, she turned the phone over to Bert.

"There is nothing of importance to the business left in the house," said Bert. "The attorneys say to stay out of their way. If they can find anything useful on the murder, fine. If I'm not there, I won't have to produce documentation to back up anything I might say. Sorry, to leave you in the line of fire. Have they questioned why you're back in town?"

"Apparently, no one has thought of that yet. I'll just have to tell them I couldn't stay away from Mrs. Bruckner's cooking. Have you been able to make any progress on her case with the INS?"

"No. I'd get more results talking to a burro than a bureaucrat. They say the case is pending and they won't discuss it at this time. But, I suspect the decision has been made and they don't want any interference."

The conversation was interrupted by Fuente returning. "They're finished in the house, but it will take some time to work the exterior. I'm to take you in for an interview."

Sage tried to say he'd drive in to the office, but Fuente wouldn't hear of it. Sage tried to make arrangements for Bert to pick him up. Fuente maintained it wouldn't be necessary. Before long Sage found himself locked in number five, the same little interrogation room he'd been in before. A clock somewhere was tolling noon.

An hour later, Sage was still waiting. Two hours later he pounded on the door but no one answered his efforts. By three he had to go to the bathroom. Still no one came. Turning his back to the mirror, which was probably a one-way glass, Sage pissed on the table leg. Then he pulled his chair into the corner so he couldn't be seen from the window. With considerable self-control he got his anger under wraps. That was what the sheriff wanted....to upset him. He decided he would play the waiting game. He wouldn't let that bastard ruffle him. That didn't mean he couldn't plot. The first subject that came to mind was that if they left him in there until he had to pee again he'd see if he could short out the electrical panel mounted in the wall. I might be an interesting challenge to see if he could do so without getting himself shocked.

He had opportunities to work on the electrical panel a couple of times before a deputy, whom Sage didn't recognize, came to fetch him at 10:00 pm. His excuse was that the sheriff had gotten tied up and couldn't get in to see him. The interview would have to be rescheduled.

Sage had missed lunch and dinner. There hadn't been anything to eat or drink. But, Sage was still playing the game. He didn't comment or complain about his treatment. He had nothing to say as the deputy drove him back to the Brand place.

When Sage let himself in through the alarm system, Mrs. Bruckner didn't put in an appearance. He didn't want to go out on the streets to get something to eat, where the sheriff or his cohorts might get another crack at him....so he raided the refrigerator. He made a stack of sandwiches from some leftover sauerbraten. He found an open bottle of red wine.

For the next two days, Sage carefully cleaned all the soot off the painting. Bert was away on business. Each day, a sheriff's unmarked car came by. Mrs. Bruckner had been instructed to disappear as soon as a car came into the yard. No one could see Sage's car in the garage and he didn't come down from the second floor. After getting no answer at the door, the car left.

On the second afternoon, Sage got a call on his cell phone from the DNA lab. When contact was established, Doctor Randall came on the line. "You were right, the DNA from the urine and the hair sample are from the same person. You were lucky. Not always is it possible to get DNA from urine and that is because it may   contain certain elements that degrade easily without proper storage. Time is also an element. However, the urine sample also   contained detritus from a menstrual cycle. That made the comparison possible.

When we saw the similarity in the characteristics of the known hair sample you brought in, to the ones we were processing, we pushed on through with the third item. We have a positive match on all three samples coming from the same source. In the hair samples, there are all sorts of other matching characteristics such as bleach, coloring and certain dietary items that leave traces. Where do you want the reports sent?"

"Hang onto the reports for the moment. Unless I tell you otherwise, I will have a guy named Tiny, pick up one copy when it is needed. Tiny is anything but tiny. So if a mountain walks in the door and says he's Tiny, give him a report."

After Sage hung up, he sat back for a bit to go over the ramifications of the known elements. Caliwildflower was the person in the secret room. The yellow ochre stain wasn't there the day of the murder. The next morning the body was discovered and from that time on, there was no way she could have gotten into the room to leave the stain that he'd found when he was able to get back into the house. The house was under constant guard. The gun may establish even more if she left fingerprints on it.

If Caliwildflower is the murderer, then Elke must be implicated. Caliwildflower was in the house the night Elke messed with his painting, but she couldn't have seen Brand open the room because he was out of town then. It may be that she had been in the house at some other time and observed something, but the chances are that Elke found out about the room and told the tree-hugger. In fact, the night Elke damaged his painting, she could have shown off the room.

Sage wondered if the plight of the black-tailed prairie dog was enough to commit murder, or did Elke have an agenda of her own? The pair were probably still lurking somewhere around the area waiting for a chance to get into the room. They were probably well aware that the sheriff hadn't found anything incriminating or he'd have been looking for them.

Sage decided to let someone else determine the motive. He put in a call for Bert. Mrs. Mills said that Bert was getting back to town that evening and she'd have him call.

Next Sage, called Tiny. "Tiny, this is Sage. Tell the boss that the reports are in and they are as I had hoped. We need to meet tonight....a very private meeting. Call me."

A few minutes later Tiny called back. "Go to dinner at Pissaro's on Fifth. Park in the public lot next to the building. At 7:00 go across the street to the Roxie....it's one of those big budget ScFi action flicks. Someone will take you out the back door and you'll be picked up."

Bert hadn't called back yet, so Sage phoned his wife with instructions for Bert to drop by the Brand house in the morning. On the way out, he checked to make sure the security guards were on duty. He flipped the switch to activate the bug before heading for dinner.

Following the directions, at 7:05 Sage found himself sitting beside Roskal in a classic Continental. "You had someone show up at the restaurant. He's still sitting watching your car and the theater," said the union boss.

"They don't have to follow me. With that GPS they can tell where I go and move in when I stop." Bastards.

"Whatcha got for me? Those labs aren't cheap. This better be worthwhile."

"I don't know what you consider worthwhile, but if you want to get Swain off your back, I can do that. It would also tickle my fancy if we could make Swain look like a blithering idiot."

Even in the dim light, Sage could see the leer come over Roskal's face at that thought.

"How's your relationship with Lawrence Webster, District Attorney?"

"He's another politician who wants union support and money. Politicians are all about the same."

"Would you favor him over Swain as governor?"

"Anyone but that prick Swain."

"All right, then how would you like to bypass Swain and give Webster the Brand murderer?"

"You know who killed Brand?"

"I think I do, but in any case what I have will prove that it wasn't either of us. You're a big wheel around here. If you called a press conference, do you think you could attract the major media and also get the DA to attend without alerting Swain?"

"Depends on what I've got."

"Let me tell you a story." Sage laid out how he'd found the yellow ochre stain on the floor and his subsequent inquiries that had revealed the secret room. He showed Roskal some of the photos of the interior of the room and pointed out what he had found.

"The testing you paid for was to match the urine I wiped up with the hair from the Velcro. We have a positive match. The other sample I took to the lab was another hair from a brush in the master bedroom. It matches the DNA from the secret room."

Sage then built the probable case against Caliwildflower and Elke starting with his recognition of the yellow haired woman on TV in Texas. Roskal got a chuckle out of the mock photo of the prairie dogs in a cage.

Roskal knew there had been a fire at the Brand house, but he had no further information. After hearing about the photo being sent to Elke, he concurred it was probably those two that tried to incinerate the evidence.

When Sage finished his story, the two got down to the serious business of plotting.

Tiny had Sage back to the theater in time for him to leave with the crowd. Sage headed home with only a stop at a liquor store to get the makings for a martini.

Bert was at the house by 9:00 am. Over breakfast, Sage related the events of the preceding evening. He was having fun. Bert was relieved to be reasonably assured that Dieter's killer would be brought to trial. In his own mind, all the facts pointed to the environmentalist. At the same time, he was saddened to think that one of the kids who had grown up in the house during his employment with Dieter would be involved in his cold-blooded murder.

Although no time had been set yet, Bert knew that there was

going to be a lot more traffic through the house. He got Mrs. Bruckner to help secure valuables and lock rooms that were not involved in the activities. All the while, he was trying to figure out how to tell Mrs. Bruckner, who had helped raise the Brand kids since they were little guys, that Elke was involved in her father's murder. He couldn't say anything yet, but he was going to have to explain it to her after it became public knowledge.

Tiny called at 11:15 am and then handed his phone to Roskal. "The announcement is set for 2:00 pm today at the Longshoreman Union Hall. Tiny picked up a report from the lab. It's as you said. The DA will be there. He'd better be, if he ever wants to run for governor. Leave those wheels of yours home. They're too conspicuous. I'll send someone for you at 1:00."

Exactly at 2:00 pm Anthony Roskal came striding out of the wings onto the stage at the front of the huge union meeting hall. The podium was wired for sound and the various members of the media had added their own mikes. There was a good turnout of print people as well. Sage wondered what Roskal had said to get such a good turnout.

Tiny was lurking in the background. Seated at the end of the front row, away from the knot of reporters was the DA, Webster. He was getting some curious looks from the various news people, but no one went to question him with Roskal taking the stage. Sage, standing at the rear of the room didn't rate any attention. Maybe the news people thought he was the janitor.

After testing the PA mike, Roskal began, "Thank you ladies and gentlemen for turning out with such short notice. I have an important matter that has just come to my attention, which needs to be handled properly.

"Let me back up a bit to review some recent history. Most of you folks have covered the dispute that arose when Dieter Brand announced plans to build a super port just south of here. The developer and the union got into a big argument concerning the new technology that was proposed. As you know, I objected on the grounds that longshoreman jobs would be lost and the little guy shoved out. That battle became heated at times. Then Dieter

Brand was murdered. Because of our business disputes, Sheriff Harvey L. Swain immediately put me at the head of his list of suspects and then used that as a pretext to go on a fishing trip to snoop into my professional activities, my private life, and the affairs of the Longshoreman's Union.

"I have not been the only one to suffer from Sheriff Swain's incompetence. Since his investigation had turned up nothing to point to a real suspect, he continues to make life miserable for those around the victim. The artist who was working in the house at the time of the murder is a queer in the sheriff's book. All artists are queer according to Swain. So the artist suffers all sorts of indignities including having his classic car reduced to buckets of nuts and bolts looking for something that existed only in the sheriff's head.

"Anyway after weeks of intensive investigation, Sheriff Swain has no clue as to who murdered one of our prominent citizens. Oh, yes, even though we had our disputes, Dieter Brand was one of the primary movers for a brighter future in this state.

"The sheriff has been ineffectual in finding the murderer. So to get him off the backs of the innocent, the ridiculed and defamed artist did the work that the sheriff and all his highly paid forensic experts have failed to do....give us a real suspect.

"Sage Grayling has given us that suspect. Now it is up to the government to build the case and get the conviction. Since the sheriff has proven himself to be incompetent in this matter, I have asked the District Attorney, Lawrence G. Webster to come down to receive the collected evidence and direct the investigation. Mr. Webster has assured me that he has available to him the services of the State Crime Lab to help develop the physical evidence of this case. Mr. Webster, please."

District Attorney Webster rose and went up onto the stage. All cameras shifted to follow his approach to the podium. The two men shook hands. Roskal extended a large envelope saying, "This is a DNA report on two specimens that came from a secret room that Mr. Grayling found. The two specimens match as being from the same person. He also had tested a known sample from another source, and the DNA matches the ones found in the room.

"Mr. Grayling has in his possession a footprint taken off the floor of that room. It is believed, but not proven, to belong to the same person. He will turn it over to whomever you designate to preserve the line, chain, whatever it is, of evidence.

"Furthermore, here are some prints from digital photos taken in the room. One of them shows a small caliber revolver lying on a shelf. It may turn out to be the murder weapon. It has not been touched. Once we conclude here, Mr. Grayling will show you the room and how to get into it. He also has additional information which might shed light on this case."

Turning back to the media, Roskal smiled. "You may find this press conference a little strange. But, under the circumstances when we find the chief law enforcement agent of the county using his position and authority to mount a drive for higher political office instead of paying attention to the duties for which he was elected, or spending his resources satisfying petty vendettas, something different must be done. Probably, the Sheriff's Office is a competent organization, staffed with professional officers, but if the boss has another agenda, the mission suffers. Based on my personal experiences, I have concluded that Sheriff Harvey Swain is not qualified to hold public office. I have consulted with my political allies and we have decided that the labor movement will not support or fund any candidacy of Harvey L. Swain."

While Roskal was making his announcement, Webster and Sage had been having a conversation off to the rear. Webster made a couple of calls on his cell phone. When Roskal stopped to take a breath, the media started jumping out of their shorts trying to get questions answered. Their more immediate interest was on the Brand murder. Questions were being shouted at Roskal, Webster and Grayling.

The District Attorney stepped before the mikes. "You folks know as much about the new developments in the Brand murder as I do, so I can't answer any questions pertaining to that case. I have ordered Mr. Grayling not to discuss his discoveries until we have had a chance to get his statements. About the only thing I can tell you is that I have asked the State Crime Lab to help with the forensic work needed in this case. I have deputy district attorneys currently securing the scene to prevent unauthorized entry. When we leave here, Mr. Grayling will show us the evidence he has found. Should the evidence be sufficient, my office will issue any necessary warrants. Thank you."

The District Attorney and his entourage, including Sage, departed through the rear of the room leaving Roskal to field the questions of those few reporters who had remained. Most were making a wild dash for their trucks and cars to get to the Brand house.

During the drive back to the murder scene, Sage gave the district attorney the background of his involvement. Webster had witnessed the initial skirmish between Sage and Swain when he'd walked up the stairs the morning the body was found. Sage framed his narrative in a chronological form only leaving out the burglary in his own house, which he'd tied to Roskal. As Sage progressed through his story, the attorney kept pointing out conditions that might have contaminated various pieces of evidence. He also pointed out various actions where Swain, then the investigation officer, could hold Sage legally liable to such charges as concealing evidence or giving false testimony. "Under the circumstances I wouldn't think he'd try to press any charges, because he'd have to come through me to get the complaints.... but he's been known to pull some pretty stupid stunts." A sly smile moved the jowls.

You're just a slimy politician too, but at the moment you are the lesser of two evils, thought Sage.

A considerable crowd had gathered outside the gate to the Brand house. The newsmen were clamoring with questions. The TV trucks drivers were vying for space to set up their dishes. The entry was blocked by deputy DAs who were keeping everyone out. There were two Sheriff's Office cars pulled off the road. Webster was passed right through. No one had entered the house pending the DA's arrival. Bert was standing in the front doorway. Before he would admit anyone, he said he had to have a word with Sage.

Bert shut the door on the crowd. "Not long after that press conference started, INS showed up here with warrants for Mrs. Bruckner. They said the sheriff had released his hold on her. She was scooped up with her apron on and out the door. That bastard is exacting his revenge. I have the attorneys working on it, but immigration isn't listening. They will try to get a court order, but apparently Swain controls certain judges. Watch yourself."

Sage didn't have time to seethe, because Webster was eager to get on with the crucifixion of Swain. Sage led a line of men up the stairs. In the lead was Webster, followed by two deputy DAs. They were followed by the head of the State Crime Lab. Behind him were four lab techs. The last was the publicity photographer for the District Attorney's office.

The large office had been put back into its normal arrangement after Sage had cleaned the smoke from the fire off his painting. "This is the way the room looked before I started on the painting. After I started the painting, I had a lot of painting material scattered around and there were ladders and bars that changed position several times a day. I can provide you with a picture of the arrangement of my materials and equipment when the murder took place. This room was declared a crime scene following the murder. I was banned from this room until the sheriff raised the restriction. At that time, I came back to clean up the mess he had made of my work. I can also provide you with a picture of the damage....and a bill to the county for the cleanup."

Sage walked to the right edge of the painting. Pointing to the floor, he said, "When I resumed my work I found a yellow ochre colored stain on the white tile in the corner." He related how he had blamed it on a cat or dog until he found out there was none in the house. He took his audience through the thought process of it leaking out from under the wall and the subsequent testing. He touched on what he learned from Heinz. Sage tried to turn the nut, but it was too tight, just as it was supposed to be. He pulled out a pair of pliers he had hidden behind the fender in the fireplace. "I put these here this morning so I could open the room."

He backed off the nut and stepped to the painting to shove the door in. Everyone started to crowd around until Webster barked at them. Sage stepped in far enough to turn on the light.

"I need to point out some things before anyone goes in. There is part of the urine stain on the floor behind the ammo box. I wiped up what leaked under the wall. I have not moved the box. Note the width of the box and it would take a narrow ass to sit on it to pee in the corner. Above the box are some cartridge belts. There are hair strands in the Velcro. I removed one, which went to the DNA lab. You will see the bare spot on the floor where I used clear tape to lift a small, bare footprint. The print is in my sketch book locked in my car. You will find a Ruger Bearcat, .22 caliber frontier model revolver on the shelf about six feet up. I did not touch the gun. I moved the right-hand box to its current location to be able to see the gun."

"Okay," said Webster, "you have been bouncing all around it. Who is this suspect you have? How did you link her up with the murder?"

"While I was working on the painting, I was staying in the house. One night when I came back from dinner I found the painting had been damaged by Elke Brand, the murdered man's daughter. She had a friend staying with her in the master bedroom. I only saw a face with a towel wrapped around her hair. Later, after finding this room, I figured it had to be a small, blonde woman. I was watching TV at home when I saw a news story concerning a protest to protect the black-tailed prairie dog. I recognized the face as belonging to the friend of Elke. You probably all know her as Caliwildflower, the woman who spent two years sitting in a tree up the coast from here. Her real name is Elizabeth Wren. I'm certain you have ample information on her because she has been arrested numerous times for her ecological activities.

"You'll probably find her and Elke somewhere around LA. I think they tried to burn down the house the other night. That fire started right under this room.

"Come with me and I'll show you the hair brush where I got

the sample for the DNA test. Yes, I know it could be that some unknown blonde murderer stopped to brush her hair between the time she sneaked into the house before the alarm was set in the evening and tippy-toed out after the alarm was turned off in the morning. As far as I am concerned, it is now up to you experts to find the killer and get a conviction."

For the next four hours, Sage sat in the dining room dictating a statement to the male deputy DA concerning his actions and his reasoning for those actions. In certain areas, he hedged, not wanting to admit to any obvious breaches of the law. About two hours into the session, one of the techs came down to report that they had found an abundance of prints, which had been compared to file prints of Elizabeth Wren. They matched.

Webster had been wandering in and out of the room during the taking of the statement. He didn't participate in the questioning, but he would occasionally pass a note to the interrogator with a point he wanted expanded. On one visit, after the announcement of the fingerprint match, Webster interrupted the session to say an all points bulletin had been issued for the arrest of Wren and the detention of Elke for questioning.

At 7:00 pm someone brought in a mountain of hamburgers. Sage went to the kitchen to brew coffee for the crew. Once their immediate hunger had been satisfied, the investigation resumed. The crews upstairs were winding down. To secure the secret room, the doors into the large office were locked with the key and also a padlocked chain was wrapped around the door knobs. Tape was stuck across the split in the double door. The door into Brand's bedroom was also locked and taped.

Chapter 11

It was 9:00 pm by the time everyone had left. The DA had placed guards outside the house, so Bert released the private guards. When things settled down, Bert produced a bottle of Chivas Regal and a couple of glasses. "Bring your drink. I want to show you something."

Sage followed Bert through the kitchen to Mrs. Bruckner's small apartment. Sitting in a corner facing the center of the living room was an armoire. When Bert opened the double doors, a light came on. The top half was an open area and the lower portion had several drawers. Hanging on the back wall of the cabinet were two black framed photographs of smiling young men in military uniforms. Sage bent closer to see better. Both were Marines. Beneath the left photo was a presentation case with a silver star. Under the other Marine were two bronze stars and other ribbons Sage didn't recognize. The sides of the cabinet were filled with montages of photos of the boys in the various stages of growing into manhood.

"Who are these guys?"

Bert shook his head. "Anne told me that she had two sons,

155

but they had both died. It was obvious that it was a very tender subject and I didn't press. I figured that when she felt like talking about it, she would. For some reason I had the impression they had been little tykes when they died. I had no idea they were adults. Never did she indicate they were in the military.

"When immigration snatched her out of here, she only had a chance to grab her purse off the cabinet. There were two aggressive guys and an iron-pants bitch and they weren't going to be denied. After they left, I came in here to see if I could collect some clothes for her. I was going to have my wife come over to pack a bag, but because of what was going on outside I decided to defer that until later. If I couldn't get her released, I planned on sending her belongings to her when she reached her destination. I was looking around to see what there was stored when I came across this.

"I'm afraid I got nosey. I went through the drawers. They are loaded with bundles of letters, clippings and official records of various kinds. Everything is neatly packed in good old German order.

"Both Kevin and Nick were killed in Vietnam only a few weeks apart. That was before Anna came to work here. I haven't been able to figure out certain things. I had thought Bruckner was her married name, but apparently it's her maiden name. The boys carried the Bruckner name because no father is listed on their birth certificates. Certain other documents pertaining to the boys give Bruckner as the deceased father's name."

Sage's artist's eye had been going over the photographs. "I'd bet the boys favored their father. I don't see much of their mother in them. I'd also bet that both of them had the same father."

"Anna sporadically kept a diary. She must have written down important dates and events. I can read the dates, but the rest of it is in German. It goes back to before she left the old country. I think you should go through it to see if there is anything we can use to keep those bastards from deporting her." As Bert handed Sage a hardbound book about the dimensions of a standard letter, he added, "I've got to get home."

The two men retreated to the kitchen. Sage refilled his glass, and tucked the diary under his arm while he deactivated the alarm so Bert could leave.

The next morning, Sage was groping around the kitchen trying to make some coffee and a piece of toast when Bert came in.

"You look like hell, young man."

"I spent most of the night deciphering that damn diary. I'm not too sharp on the German script forms. I had to figure out her handwriting before I could even start. Then I began getting the drift of a most amazing tale."

"You sit and talk while I do the kitchen work."

"Thank you," said Sage as he slid onto a stool at the counter. "You already know most of the early part of the story. That crumb disappeared leaving Anna with two infant boys.

"She raised the boys on her own, doing housework. As soon as the younger one got old enough to enlist, both the boys joined the Marine Corps. There was no question about citizenship because they had birth certificates. Anna always stayed in the background because she was an illegal alien. She is deathly afraid of government. She has never gotten a social security number. She has never voted or participated even in any German social society group. As far as I can tell, she never even collected the GI insurance when her sons were killed in the line of duty in Vietnam. She mourned them in silence."

Bert had stopped working while listening to the story. Sage had to ask for a cup of coffee to get him moving again.

"I had no idea of her background," said Bert. "I figured she didn't have proper papers. Dieter was the kind who would help someone in need without asking for particulars. Surely, the government couldn't deport her after she sacrificed both her sons to protect this country."

"You have a higher opinion of what governmental bureaucrats will do than I. This whole thing was set up by that damned sheriff. He knows someone who'll do his bidding. That someone has the power, and nothing but a court order or a bullet in a bureaucrat's pea brain will stop him. You'd better get your attorneys to humpin' or she'll be gone before you can get through the snail-paced court system."

Through the silent house came the faint ringing of a cell phone. Sage made a dash for the bedroom, but he was too slow. His Caller ID service showed that Tiny had called. When he got through to Tiny, all the big guy had to say was, "The boss says watch the FOX news."

In Bert's office they tuned his little TV set to the designated channel. A young woman with an Indian or Pakistani name was hiding her pretty face behind a big FOX mike. To her rear was a large contingent of young, motley-dressed anarchists sitting on the ground with interlocked arms encircling a craggy, dead tree. Well above the ground was an old, worn platform guyed to the tree by numerous, frayed ropes. Tatters of blue and green canvas fluttered in a stiff breeze. Even before the camera focused on the figures on the platform, Sage knew that they were Caliwildflower and Elke Brand. He recognized their shapes. He also knew the TV feed was coming from along the coast in Ventura County where Caliwildflower had tree-sat for two years. He'd heard that the tree had been spiked and killed.

There was a vacant stretch of ground between the demonstrators and a line of deputies who were inside a strip of yellow plastic tape that was designed to keep the media and the curious public at bay.

The commentator was reviewing the chain of events for people just joining the cable channel. She said that the various news agencies had been called by Caliwildflower, a well known environmental activist, who announced that she would be holding a news conference at her sacred tree at 10:00 am. By that time, the media knew that there was a warrant out for her arrest in connection with the Brand murder. She had also invited the various local law enforcement agencies just in case someone wanted to try serving a warrant on her. The Sheriff's Office had raced to the scene trying to get her before a crowd arrived, but she was already surrounded by a couple of hundred anarchists who had rallied to her earlier calls. They formed a phalanx around the base of the tree that clung to the lip of a two-hundred foot cliff. At the bottom of the cliff was a jumble of large rocks. Beyond the rock fall was a narrow inlet with the water alternately rising and falling from wave action.

The camera panned around toward the entrance to the area. The access road was well out of sight beyond the trees. A sizeable crowd had already gathered, and dozens more could be seen moving up the hill through the trees. It was becoming a large event. Both Caliwildflower and Elke were leaning over the edge of the platform shouting and waving to various people in the assembling crowd. Communication was difficult because the police line was keeping the throngs at a considerable distance. Also the breeze was whipping any words off to the side.

A police spokesman was trying to get Caliwildflower's attention with a bull horn, but she continued to ignore him. It was obvious that the police were not going to force any issue with such a large crowd that was generally sympathetic to the environmentalists.

"Those deputies had better be calling for backup," said Sage. "They are horribly out-manned if things were to get ugly. They're in the middle of a hostile force and a long way from their cars."

"Why did they call this thing anyway....To make a political statement before surrendering?"

"No, I think they want some sort of confrontation. She wants to have one more fifteen-minutes-of-glory."

Caliwildflower surveyed the crowd. She consulted with Elke before standing up with her arms raised above her head. "Welcome, friends and enemies....Friends of Mother Earth and enemies of Mother Earth." There was a cheer. She was screaming to be heard, but only bits and pieces were coming over the microphone. Her voice was proportional to her size. The announcer had apparently gotten word that the comments weren't coming through, so she was trying to paraphrase those portions of the comments she could understand. It was a rather disjointed tirade covering the damage modern society is doing to Mother Earth. She swore an everlasting vendetta on whoever killed her beloved tree. She stepped over to the trunk and hugged it. Then she made comments about wicked industrialists killing the animals by uncontrolled development destroying their habitat. She talked about the black-tailed prairie dogs of Texas that were being brought to the edge of extinction by the likes of that land baron, Dieter Brand, and that he had gotten what he so well deserved.

Sage was straining to hear the full text. He wondered if this was going to be some sort of public confession. But from what he could understand, she only expressed satisfaction on Brand's demise without admitting to the murder.

During the whole diatribe, Elke sat with her back against the tree trunk. Her knees were drawn up under her chin. She had her arms wrapped around her legs. She didn't seem to be following her companion's denouncements.

Suddenly Caliwildflower pointed down the hill. "See, it takes a whole army to take one noble warrior in Mother Earth's army."

The camera swung around toward an advancing wedge of deputies outfitted in riot gear. They wore helmets with plastic faceplates. They carried clear plastic shields and long night sticks. The deputies stopped short of the assembled spectators, whose numbers had grown to two or three hundred people, forming a half circle around the tree. They took a more casual stance, as if waiting for orders.

The deputy with the bullhorn took advantage of the silence accompanying the arrival of the riot squad. "Miss Wren, you have had your say. Now it is time to come down and put an end to this before someone gets hurt. You know we have a warrant for your arrest for the murder of Dieter Brand."

A roar went up from the anarchists. Most of the crowd joined in. Then someone began the chant, "Cali, Cali, Cali." The rest of the assembled sympathizers took up the chant.

On the platform, Caliwildflower was prodding Elke to her feet. The two women stood shoulder to shoulder and faced the crowd, joining their inside hands. They raised the clasped hands above their heads, saluting the crowd. In slow motion they wheeled 180 degrees so they were facing the inlet. Both took one stride with the inside feet to the edge of the platform and Califwildflower took a second step off into space. Elke hesitated. As Caliwildflower plunged into space she held onto Elke's hand, jerking her over the edge. Elke flailed her right arm out, wrapping it around one of the guy ropes bringing her fall to an abrupt halt, ripping their hands apart. Caliwildflower's scream "Elkeeeeeeeeeee" pierced the air. Elke was left dangling in air with her right elbow hooked in the rope.

A great cheer went up from the anarchists who stood and saluted with their fists in the air. There were some cheers from the crowd, but mostly screams. The riot deputies cut loose with several compressed air horns, which blasted the crowd aside as the wedge charged straight through the assembled supporters. Some of the anarchists tried to resist, but the deputies thrust their batons into soft spots, decreasing their will to cause trouble. The supporters couldn't retreat because of the cliff. They were divided and forced back into the surrounding crowds. The deputies in riot gear were unable to climb a rope, so two of the early arrivals shinnied up the ropes to pull Elke back up onto the platform.

One of the deputies leaned out over the cliff to look down. After a moment's consideration he turned to the deputies on the ground and shook his head.

Sage let out a deep breath. He looked at Bert who was shaking his head too. "Such a pity. She was a great kid. How can one pull such a complete reversal?"

"Since I don't have any kids, I'd have to guess. The big question now is, what are you going to do? Elke is in custody and I would imagine she is going to face life in prison, if what we surmise proves to be true."

Bert shook his head sadly. "I'll have to see that she gets adequate representation. She's pretty much alone in the world. If I know her brother, he won't want anything to do with her. She's an embarrassment to him."

"Are you sure he knew nothing about this murder?"

"No, I'm not."

Chapter 12

When the TV coverage of the big story finally started to subside, Bert took his leave. Sage was alone in that huge, luxury house. He decided it wasn't a fun place to be in without agreeable souls about. There were rent-a-guards outside to preserve the integrity of the secret room. The district attorney was now footing the bill. Apparently he didn't even trust Swain to protect evidence in a felony case.

Sage got Dreadnought out of the garage to make the trip to the Chili Bell for dinner. He was about halfway through his paella when a voice asked, "Mind if I join you?"

It was Lieutenant Fuente. "Sit. How about a Tecate?" *I thought I'd turned off that damn bug.*

"Si, como no?"

The two men hefted their cans to each other in a toast. Sage let the lieutenant open the conversation.

"I hope you aren't painting me with the same brush as Swain. I've been around here a lot longer than he. Swain was elected a couple of years ago and I've been in the department for ten. I have a career and family to protect. And just as importantly, I have a good, decent department that deserves better than what the electorate gave us. If we can weather Swain, we'll be a first-class outfit again."

"My beef is with Swain, not you or your department."

"I'd hoped that was the situation. In case you're wondering, the owner of this place is my wife's cousin. He called to say you were here. You've been the subject of several conversations in the big booth in the corner. The reason I left a really good baseball game in the seventh inning is to pass along the word that you are really on the boss's shit list. As far as he is concerned, you are the reason for his downfall. Roskal all but crushed his hopes of ever being governor of this state. He needs the union vote and financial backing even to get through the primary. Now his arch rival is going to get all that he thinks belongs to him.....and you are the culprit. I was a little suspicious about your return to LA after the painting was finished, but the reason didn't matter to the sheriff. He just wanted to administer a little more pain for your innuendos to the press. He'd been obliquely questioned about his sexual preferences."

"I'm about ready to get out of town and leave Sheriff Swain to you. I've done what I wanted to do. When I first saw him I didn't like him. At that time, I was content to stay away from anything involving him, but he made it personal by calling me a 'poof'. I might even have lumped that, but he continued to heap it on, so...."

"Well, he's still sheriff and he still wields a lot power. With the Democrats dumping him, I doubt if he can win reelection. We still have two more years of him."

Sage changed the subject. "How about Caliwildflower and Elke Brand?"

"That little episode just heaped insult onto injury as far as Swain is concerned. Webster wouldn't let him near the Brand house. He by-passed the Sheriff's Office for forensic help and even guards. Swain is absolutely beside himself. The press smelled a problem immediately and the sheriff has been trying to explain the situation ever since. No one in the department will say a word about it, but everyone refers any questions to the sheriff. He has some of his boys in the highest jobs in the department. They shield him somewhat, but the press is laying in wait to ask him embarrassing questions."

"What's happened to Elke after she turned chicken-shit and wouldn't jump?"

"She's a psychological mess. They can't shut her up. She keeps babbling on. She's told the DA all he has to know to convict her of 1st degree murder. The feeling is that she is going crazy, but at the time of the murder she was sane and that is what they need to convict."

"How did she find the room?"

"It was down in Texas, she was sneaking around as was her habit and she watched her father open the room to get a bottle of good wine. Later, she duplicated his actions and got into the room. When she went to California, the same thing worked."

"She told that tree-hugger...."

"Yeah, the two had been running around together. When Caliwildflower became interested in the black-tailed prairie dogs, Elke told her about the colony that lived on a piece of her father's property. There was a pretty extensive city there, and Caliwildflower adopted it as her new crusade."

"Yeah, there was a TV spot on her environmental crusade for the prairie dogs. That was when I made the connection between her and the yellow hair."

"Elke's father was planning on selling the property for a subdivision, which would have killed or displaced the prairie dogs. The two plotted to kill Dieter before he could do any more ecological damage. Also Elke would have all the money they needed to put a whole series of plans into effect. Elke had entered into a pact with her brother to divide up the estate. Elke would get the Texas property and Karl was to get California. When her dad was dead she planned to deed the prairie dog city over to the organization Caliwildflower was going to create."

"Did both of them come to California?"

"No, Elke stayed behind. She kept telling her interrogators that she told Cali, as Elke calls her, to put something on her feet while on the plane or somebody will report her as being weird. She laid out the whole plan for Cali. When she got here, Cali borrowed a car from a friend and drove to a secluded area behind the Brand property. She hiked over the hills and waited until the appropriate time to enter through a back door that goes to the basement. She went to the secret room and hid there until Brand was alone. She took a .22 revolver off the wall. It was loaded. She shot him and disappeared into the room, coming out in the morning after the alarm system had been turned off. You had it figured pretty well. Elke knew nothing about the puddle of urine."

"Did Cali what's-her-name return to Texas, or did Elke come here?"

"Cali returned and they stayed there until your photo came. They panicked. They both flew to California and hiked over the hills to set the fire. They sat up on the hill to await the results. When the house didn't burn, they watched for another opening to get into the room, but too many people were around."

"They still must have been in the area when Roskal had his press conference."

"Yeah, they were staying with a friend who told them about the press conference."

"That about wraps everything up, doesn't it?"

"Not quite, there's another thing. The sheriff will charge you with a whole list of things from false statements to tampering with evidence and hiding evidence of a crime. The only reason he isn't actively pursuing them at the moment is that he'd have to go up against Webster to get the charges and the DA is shielding you. But, don't press your luck."

"He can't prove any of that."

"He knows that, but he'd like nothing better than to throw you into jail for six months while you're proving your innocence. He'd probably pay some jailhouse toughs to turn you into their honey."

"A nice, fine, upright citizen you have there....and the public doesn't realize what they got when they voted for him."

"Oh, they got a Democrat win. That's all that is important to the few who take the time to vote."

Sage decided to take Fuente's warning seriously. He made sure the bug in his car was inactive before he headed to the Brand place. He stayed there only long enough to pack his things. He was on the road and out of the county in an hour. Before leaving the area, he called Bert.

"I'm on my way back to Albuquerque. Fuente looked me up at dinner and warned me Swain is out for my scalp. I'm not going to give him a chance when he holds all the cards."

Sage gave Bert the inside information on Elke that he'd learned from Fuente. Before he signed off he asked, "How are you coming with immigration?"

"I have a bunch of attorneys on it now. I was able to send her clothes to her, but they wouldn't let me see her. She is getting some special attention and I suspect it is Swain's doings. There is nothing to report at the moment. Papers are flying around."

"Please let me know what is happening. If you can get her out of jail, I'll make her disappear again."

*****

When Sage pulled into the yard, he could see Tinna's truck parked by the granary. He pulled into the garage and closed the door. From somewhere in the compound he could hear the beat of Rossini's Thieving Magpie. It always made him think of high-step marching. As he passed through the kitchen he was a little miffed that Tinna had invaded his bedroom–but the music wasn't coming from there; it was coming from the granary. As he stepped through the breezeway into the back compound, he was met with an alluring sight. Apparently he wasn't the only one that Rossini affected that way. Tinna came marching out of the granary wearing nothing but a pair of flip-flops and a towel around her neck. She was executing a fancy drum major prance, heading for the shower. When, out of the corner of her eye, she glimpsed Sage leaning against the wall, arms folded, wearing a grin a mile wide, she almost disjointed herself trying to straighten herself out.

This time it was Tinna's turn to get embarrassed. Sage gave her credit that she didn't react like a little shrinking violet and try to cover up. It wasn't her body that was causing her anguish. It was her actions that were the source of her discomfort. Now I have a "gotcha."

"Cabron, you didn't honk your horn."

"And miss this performance?"

Tinna actually blushed.

"I presume you're headed for the shower. Don't take too long. I'm mixing martinis." He stepped aside to let her pass. He followed the undulating butt until she turned into the bathroom. Stepping back to the kitchen, he quickly checked the mail. He sifted out the bills that needed immediate attention and left the rest for later.

In his bedroom, he checked the answering machine. There was nothing of any consequence there either. When he heard the shower go off, he turned his attention to the martinis. As he suspected, she made a quick trip back to the granary for shorts, tank top and sandals. When she came in the door she was smiling. Her indomitable sense of humor prevailed.

Sage handed her a martini saying, "I've never enjoyed Rossini more."

"I'll bet you've never had it performed like that. I'm glad you enjoyed it. It must be your choice in music. It's your CD. I borrowed it. I still can't find mine. They're still packed away. From what I hear, you're trip to Los Angeles must have been successful. At least, the bad guys aren't running around anymore. Was that your doing?"

"Pretty much. But there is still is another bad apple out there.... Sheriff Swain. At least he shouldn't become governor where he could do even more damage. The unions have dumped him. But again, the public doesn't know much about his antics. They may forget everything they do know in the next couple of years. If he can get any backing, he still could run."

"What are you going to do about it?"

"It's not my problem. He'll make life miserable for me if he ever can catch me in his jurisdiction. I'll just have to stay out of his way for two years."

"What happens if you get another commission in that area? Are you going to pass it up?"

"That's not likely. This was the first one I'd ever had in California."

Tinna shrugged. "Tell me what happened."

For the next couple of hours, Sage related the chronology of events. Tinna was always full of questions, so telling the story took a while. He had figured he'd go out to eat, but after the martinis, that didn't seem prudent. The two of them ended up in the kitchen making selections from the freezer.

Sage had delayed his trip to Texas for a week, so he could sort out his painting material and have time to work on Tinna's apartment. The next morning he made an attempt to get up at a reasonable hour. The only way he made it was to follow his nose to the smell of brewing coffee. Tinna still didn't have a workable kitchen so she was in his, scrambling eggs and cheese, which was folded into toasted English muffins. She'd anticipated his appearance. There were extra breakfast makin's waiting.

They took their second cups of coffee out to the granary so Sage could see what had happened during his absence. Tinna had progressed nicely. The ceiling/roof was complete. She needed some help in positioning and installing the staircase she'd hauled in so they could get to the storage area over her apartment. The T-1-11 exterior plywood was all cut and nailed. She had set two windows looking out into the granary.

Now there was a problem of insulation. The granary would get bitterly cold during the winter. The house had three-foot thick walls which made good insulation. They held their heat well into the cold season. That day, Tinna and Sage took the truck into the supply and picked up great rolls of fiberglass insulation. They stapled it in between the studs and ceiling joists. Sage decided to go with drywall for the interior finish. He had a friend who worked for a construction firm doing drywall installation. The guy wanted to be a sculptor, but he had to keep his day job. Sage called to him to install the gypsum sheets on the weekend. Sage's pay would finance a small bronze casting at the Shidoni foundry.

On the third day after his return, Sage got a call from Bert, who was beside himself. "Anna has been flown to New York awaiting her deportation to Germany. "My attorneys have been blocked all along the line. They are getting absolutely nowhere. They are up against the machine. Swain is pulling strings. He's determined to deport Anna. Now she is classified as an enemy alien, which changes her status so all the papers we've filed are useless. I'm running out of time and ammunition."

When Sage hung up he was depressed. He knew Anna Bruckner had problems because Swain wanted to hurt him, Bert, and all connected with the murder investigation. *That vindictive bastard deserves anything he gets.*

That night, he had trouble getting to sleep. In the middle of the night he awakened with his mind going at jet speed. He spent the rest of the night plotting. In the morning, he told Tinna he had some work to do in his office. When he was sure Bert was up, he called California. It took him a while to get his idea across because he didn't want to involve Bert in any more of his scheme than was necessary. He wanted Bert to be able to proclaim his ignorance.

After he hung up, he refreshed his coffee while waiting for a return call. He didn't have long to wait for Bert's call to give him a phone number. It was for Zip, the nerd that had designed the computer system to move freight around a proposed new port.

Zip was awaiting his call. "Hey, man, I hear ya got something that might be fun to do. I need a break. I'm dying in commercial boredom. Whatcha' want?"

It took some time to get the whole program across. In the end, Zip was chortling and cooing over the delicious prospects. Sage had to promise to give him a blow-by-blow report on the outcome.

Now that the plotting was over, his mind slowed down. He went out to find Tinna to tell her he was going to take a nap and then head for LA again. He gave her a brief report on what he hoped to accomplish.

"Now this is what I call an 'absentee landlord.' Good luck."

The road to LA was getting all too familiar. He got to the coast in the late afternoon. He pulled into a cafe for a rest stop and a drink. Before getting on the road again, he called Tiny, who turned his phone over to the boss.

After the preliminaries, Sage got down to business. "Hey, Tony. I got Swain off your back and out of your business. I simplified your political agenda by eliminating one of your bad apples from trying to get backing. I also enhanced your standing as a powerful union leader and so on. In my book, you owe me a favor."

"What kind of favor?" said Roskal, suspiciously.

"A man in your position obviously collects a whole bunch of friends and acquaintances in high places. I would guess that some of these acquaintances owe you some deference because of your help in getting them into the exalted positions they hold. If that is the case, then they should not hesitate a bit in helping you do a great service for this country in righting a grievous wrong that is being committed as we speak."

"Go on."

"Where were you born?"

"Here."

"Your parents?

"The old country. Where is this going?"

"Swain is trying to get even with me and Bert Mills. To do so, he has reported Anna Bruckner, Brand's long-time cook and house domo, to the INS. She was brought into this country by a GI with a hard cock, who turned out to be a weak-kneed idiot who wouldn't break with church and family to marry her. He did sneak away twice....long enough to get her pregnant. On her own hook, she raised two sons who turned out to be decorated heroes....dead decorated heroes....in Vietnam.

"Because of her legal status, she has kept all of this secret. In her room is a tiny shrine to her two boys. Bert found it after INS scooped her up in order to deport her back to Germany. They took her with nothing more than the clothes and the apron she wore. Bert also found the histories of their lives when he went to get some clothes to send to her in jail.

"Swain is managing this action so that Brand's attorneys can't even file papers in the appropriate spot before the situation changes.

"My favor is that you get in contact with those high-powered politicos who owe you some consideration for their lofty status. I want Anna Bruckner released from custody and given a legal status so she can come out into the sunlight after decades of hiding. She should be honored as the mother of American silver and double bronze star heroes. I rather doubt she even collected her sons' GI life insurance. Think of how your mother would have felt to be sent back to the old country after spending four decades or so here.

"This country owes her. I remember my parents talking about the Gold Star Mothers in World War II. A lot of houses down the street had little placards in the window with a Gold Star. That told the world they had lost a son in defense of our country. Occasionally, a window had two stars. That was a family to be cherished."

"Okay, I'll see what I can do. I can't promise anything. Some of those big boys forget where they came from. I'll get back to you. Where are ya?"

"I'm in LA right now. As soon as I can deliver a little surprise to Swain, I'll head back home. I still have to paint another scene in Brand's Texas house. Tiny has my cell phone number."

"What are you going to do to Swain?"

"If I can pull it off, you'll hear about it. If I don't, I may be calling for help getting out of jail."

Next, he called Zip to make arrangements for a meeting to pick up an envelope. It took a little time to track Fuente down. When he finally made contact, he suggested it might be in the department's interest to make the sheriff aware that the bug in Sage's car was sending in a signal. Then Sage suggested Fuente disappear for the evening.

Before he turned on the bug he made his rendezvous with Zip. *What a crazy, irreverent, likeable guy.*

Sage turned on Dreadnought's bug and consulted a map on how to get to the longshoreman's union hall. When he'd been there earlier, he'd noted a Greek restaurant right next door. Sage decided it would make an excellent added feature for Swain if he thought there might be something going on between Sage and Roskal. He parked Dreadnought in the street right in front of the restaurant so he could see it through the window. Sage was halfway through his Greek salad when suddenly he was surrounded by plainclothes deputies. They hadn't drawn any guns, but their hands were not far away. It was the young, numb-skull deputy, Huxley, the first to arrive at the Brand house after the murder, who stepped forward to recite the Miranda rights. He stuck out his puny chest, cleared his throat and told Sage he was being taken in on suspicion of dealing in drugs and possession of drug paraphernalia.

Sage poured a little more dressing on his salad as he swallowed a bite. "Bullshit."

Huxley bristled and moved his hand closer to his gun.

Sage looked at him in contempt. "Are you going to shoot me because I'm wielding a wicked salad fork? Before you get yourself deeper in an illegal action, look at what is in that envelope."

Huxley stepped close enough to quickly pluck the envelope from the table. He pulled out three folded letter-sized computer pages. A flicker of distaste moved across his face as he shuffled through the papers. "What's this all about?"

"You tell Swain he'd better get down here before I finish my meal or he will spend the rest of his life labeled a sexual predator." Sage shifted his attention away from the surrounding deputies back to his plate. He took another bite of salad.

The other deputies were craning their necks to see the sheets. Huxley refolded them and stuck the papers in his jacket pocket. He told the three other deputies, "Keep him here." Huxley stepped out the door.

A man, who Sage presumed was the owner of the restaurant, was trying to muster enough courage to try finding out what was happening. He nervously shifted from foot to foot. There were a half a dozen tables with curious patrons. Sage was glad to have so many witnesses.

Addressing the owner, Sage said loudly, "Sorry for the incident. Sheriff Swain will be along shortly to clear up a misunderstanding." Sage went back to his salad. The deputies backed off a little, but remained vigilante. They were concerned. Probably they feared the sheriff and that they were not doing as he had ordered. They would feel his wrath.

When Huxley came back in, he said, "The sheriff's coming," before backing off to join the other deputies.

Sage held up his empty salad plate. The waiter removed the dirty dish and quickly returned with the entree of roast lamb.

Although his nerves were drawn absolutely rigid, he maintained a casual demeanor. He slowly made his way through the meal. He didn't know much about Greek cooking, but the lamb was tasty. He liked the touch of rosemary. He would have enjoyed it more if he hadn't been afraid that Swain wouldn't get there in time to prevent him from having to execute his threat. To extend the time, he ordered coffee and the pastry cart. He was just making a selection of baklava when the deputies shifted nervously. Sage didn't look up, but asked the waiter to bring a second cup of coffee.

Swain, in civvies, towered over Sage and in a low voice that wouldn't carry far, he hissed, "What's all this shit?"

Still, without looking up, Sage said, "Sit down and I'll tell you. Do you want a pastry too?"

Reluctantly, Swain sat. He did not want to create a scene in front of so many witnesses. As he was sitting, two more couples came into the establishment. They hesitated when they noticed the knot of men and caught the tension in the air. Sage didn't let them leave. "Come on in folks, Sheriff Swain will be through in a few minutes. Enjoy your meal."

Sage saw his opponent was about ready to erupt into action, which could well be violent. "Why don't you send those guys away? I don't think you want them to hear this."

"Hear what, you little ...."

"Poof?"

"What are you trying to pull?"

Sage looked at the nervous deputies.

Swain motioned them outside. "Now, what's this all about?"

"Those printouts are only three of dozens and dozens of similar selected photos, which are now in your computer. Oh, I know you can run home and toss that CPU in the fireplace, but a friend already has downloaded all your files with the embedded photos. They can be sent to any computer. Also, you shouldn't have left the password for your office computer in your home machine. Your office machine is also stuffed full of similar photos. And you can't toss the county computer system in the fireplace."

"What?" roared Swain as he jumped to his feet nearly knocking the table over. Sage salvaged his own cup and baklava by raising them from the erupting surface. "You couldn't...."

"Sit down. You're making a scene. Sit down or I'll let everyone in this place know about you."

Swain glanced around at all the faces turned in his direction. He sat down and snarled, "There's no way you could do that."

"Not me....but someone who really knows computers can. I didn't bother to ask how he did it. I wouldn't understand if he told me. All I wanted were results. I have them. I don't know how the courts handle pedophiles in California. In my state, the sentences are long and hard. Then, when you get out, you have to register your address with the police and in turn the police tell the neighbors, who then drive the pedophile out of their neighborhood and he has to look for other accommodations so the routine can start all over again. Also, whenever there is a child molestation case in the community, guess who gets immediate attention? Rather like the attention I've been getting. But, I don't have to tell the sheriff of a big, important county about how pedophiles are handled, do I?"

"You bastard, you can't do that."

"It's already done. Where it goes from here is up to you."

Swain was turning purple. "What do you want?"

"I want you to resign as sheriff. You're clever enough to figure out a reason. In fact, from the color of your face, you could probably claim a heart condition right now."

"Absolutely not. Those pictures aren't of me and I can prove it."

"You don't have to be in the pictures to be in possession of child porn. Some big movie star just got nailed for that the other day. You'll never be able to dump all those pictures. Someone will find one and then the search will be on. If no one stumbles on to them soon, then my friend will drop one into some clerk's active files. You don't have any time to try finding them."

"If you think you can get away with this you're sadly mistaken. I'll have your hide. You aren't the only one with high tech friends. I'll get you."

"Don't go making threats. Deviate charges can be filed while you're sheriff or when you just a plain old citizen. With a little bit more time, my friend can make it look like you're giving it to a little boy. Why are you making such a fuss? You aren't a law enforcement officer. You're only using the sheriff's job to launch your run for governor, and that's in the toilet now. Move on to other things....just don't let me ever see you again. And you'd better hope that nothing unpleasant happens to me. If anything untoward does happen to me, certain standing orders will be executed. You'd better hope no drunk driver runs me down."

Sage looked over at the other deputies huddled outside the door. "I think you'll find you've lost the support of all your flunkies. I don't think they're afraid of you anymore. The word will get around fast. Even if you were to decide to fight it and stay on, you couldn't pull all this shit anymore because they won't be afraid of you any longer."

As Sage stood up he motioned for the waiter. "The sheriff will pick up the bill. Don't forget to add your tip." Turning to the sheriff, who was so furious he was shaking, "Don't do anything foolish. You can live a long, pleasant life unless you screw with me....then what life you have will be very ugly. Think of what some of those cons would like to do to you.....especially someone who screws little boys. I'll expect to hear of your change of careers on the noon news. Oh yes, thank you for the global positioning unit in my car. I hear they're pricey." The deputies parted as Sage walked out the door.

The adrenalin was flowing. Sage knew he wouldn't be able to sleep. Also he didn't trust Swain not to come after him, so he shut off the bug and caught the closest on-ramp to a freeway that would take him out of town. He kept a sharp eye in his rear view mirror until he was out in the desert.

Sage kept the wheels rolling east until near midday, when he stopped at a motel where he could catch the news and get some much needed sleep. One of the big breaking stories was the resignation of Sheriff Harvey L. Swain for personal reasons. Sage had a smile on his face as he dropped off to sleep.

Since it was close to midnight when he pulled up to the hacienda, he honked before pulling into the garage. Tinna would probably be asleep. He didn't want her to think the house was being burglarized again if she woke up and heard him thumping and bumping around.

He put Dreadnought away and, as he entered one door to the kitchen, Tinna came in another. She was still bleary with sleep. She had a sheer robe wrapped around her. In her hand she carried herbal tea bags. "Welcome back. Give me some hot water. I can't take coffee now. If I drink these I can fall asleep after I have heard all about your wonderful adventures."

Sage put on the hot pot. He too passed on the coffee, opting for brandy. The tale lasted well into the early morning hours.

Epilogue

Tinna's apartment was coming along nicely. The drywall guy had done his job and Tinna was painting. The kitchen cabinets were in place and needed plumbing hookups. It was taking on the looks of a home. Before leaving for Texas, Sage wanted to get all the electrical finished. The toilet and the shower would have to wait for a leach field.

That was all right with Tinna. She had to turn her attention back to preparing for her big fall show. There was a lot of pottery to be constructed. She needed a break from carpentry.

One afternoon, while Sage was working under the kitchen sink, his cordless phone rang. It was Bert.

"We're in Denver waiting for a connecting flight."

"We?"

"Yes, Anna and I are flying back to LA. Your talk with Roskal paid huge dividends. In this current patriotic climate, a Senator and a Congressman teamed up to right your grievous wrong. Of course, this also gave them a chance to poke the INS in the eye. Anyway, Anna is a free woman. She has acquired a temporary legal status that will change to permanent as soon as the paperwork can be done. Anna wants to talk to you."

A flood of German came cascading down the line. Sage knew how to ask for the bread to be passed, but terms of endearment had somehow escaped him. Anyway, he got the drift of the comments, that she was ever so grateful to him and that he would remain her dear young man. Sage got the impression that he had just been adopted.

When Bert got the phone back, he said the government was making insurance payments for her two boys. There were some other benefits that would accrue to her too.

"What is she going to do now that Brand is dead?" asked Sage.

"Some decisions have been made. Dieter's house cannot be a business location because it is in a residential zoning. However, since I am now in charge of the various trusts and I will be called upon to host meetings and take care of the social obligations, I am going to move my family into the house. I will use the existing files and equipment to continue the work. Anna is going to assist around the house, freeing my wife from certain household duties so she can concentrate on being hostess for various functions. Anna will have her apartment for as long as she wants it.

"Say, the other day, the announcement came over TV that Sheriff Swain had suddenly resigned, listing personal considerations. Since then, a number of high ranking officers have also resigned. The chain of command got clear down to your friend, Lieutenant Fuente, who was appointed sheriff pro-tem until a special election can be held. Whatever you did was effective.

"We have a plane to catch. I wanted to tell you, both Anna and I are extending an unqualified invitation to you to use the Brand house as your base of operation whenever you come to LA. Thanks."

ISBN 978-0-9820044-5-6

Made in the USA
Charleston, SC
22 February 2011